BAD KITTY

Joins the Team

NICK BRUEL

SQUARE
FISH

ROARING BROOK PRESS
NEW YORK

SQUARE
FISH

An imprint of Macmillan Publishing Group, LLC
120 Broadway, New York, NY 10271
mackids.com

Our books may be purchased in bulk for promotional, educational, or business use. Please
contact your local bookseller or the Macmillan Corporate and Premium Sales Department at
(800) 221-7945 ext. 5442 or by email at MacmillanSpecialMarkets@macmillan.com.

Library of Congress Control Number: 2019941008

Originally published in the United States by Roaring Brook Press
First Square Fish edition, 2020
Book designed by Cassie Gonzales
Square Fish logo designed by Filomena Tuosto

ISBN 978-1-250-76270-2 (Square Fish paperback)
3 5 7 9 10 8 6 4 2

ISBN 978-1-250-76383-9 (special book fair edition)
1 3 5 7 9 10 8 6 4 2

AR: 3.2 / LEXILE: GN490L

• CONTENTS •

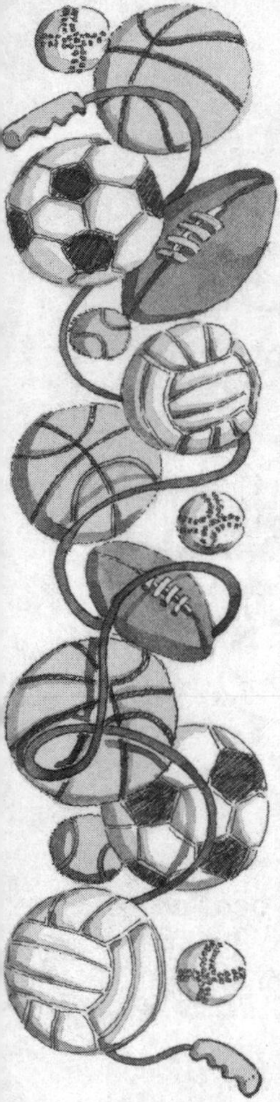

SUCH A CALM, QUIET MORNING

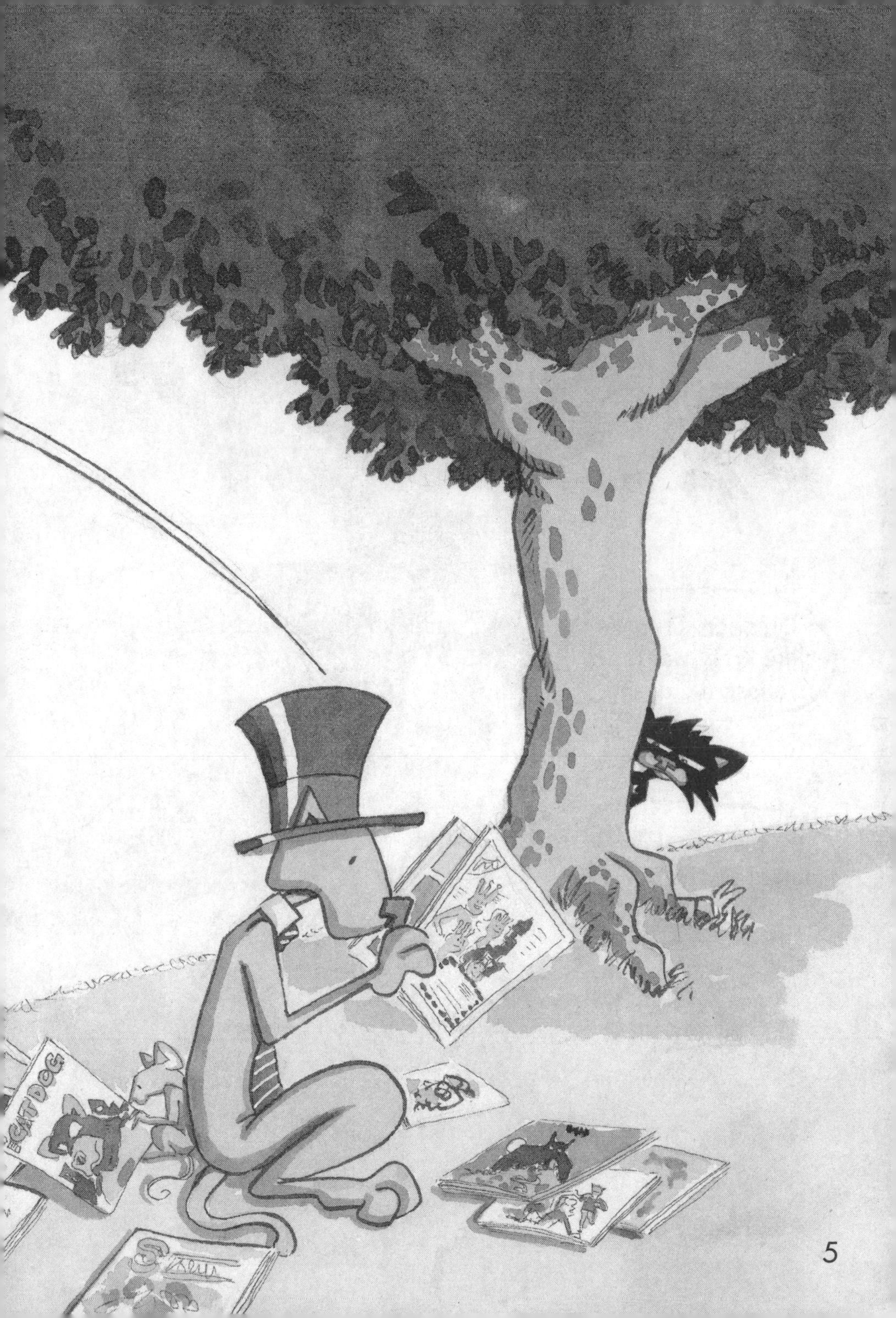
CAT DOG

6

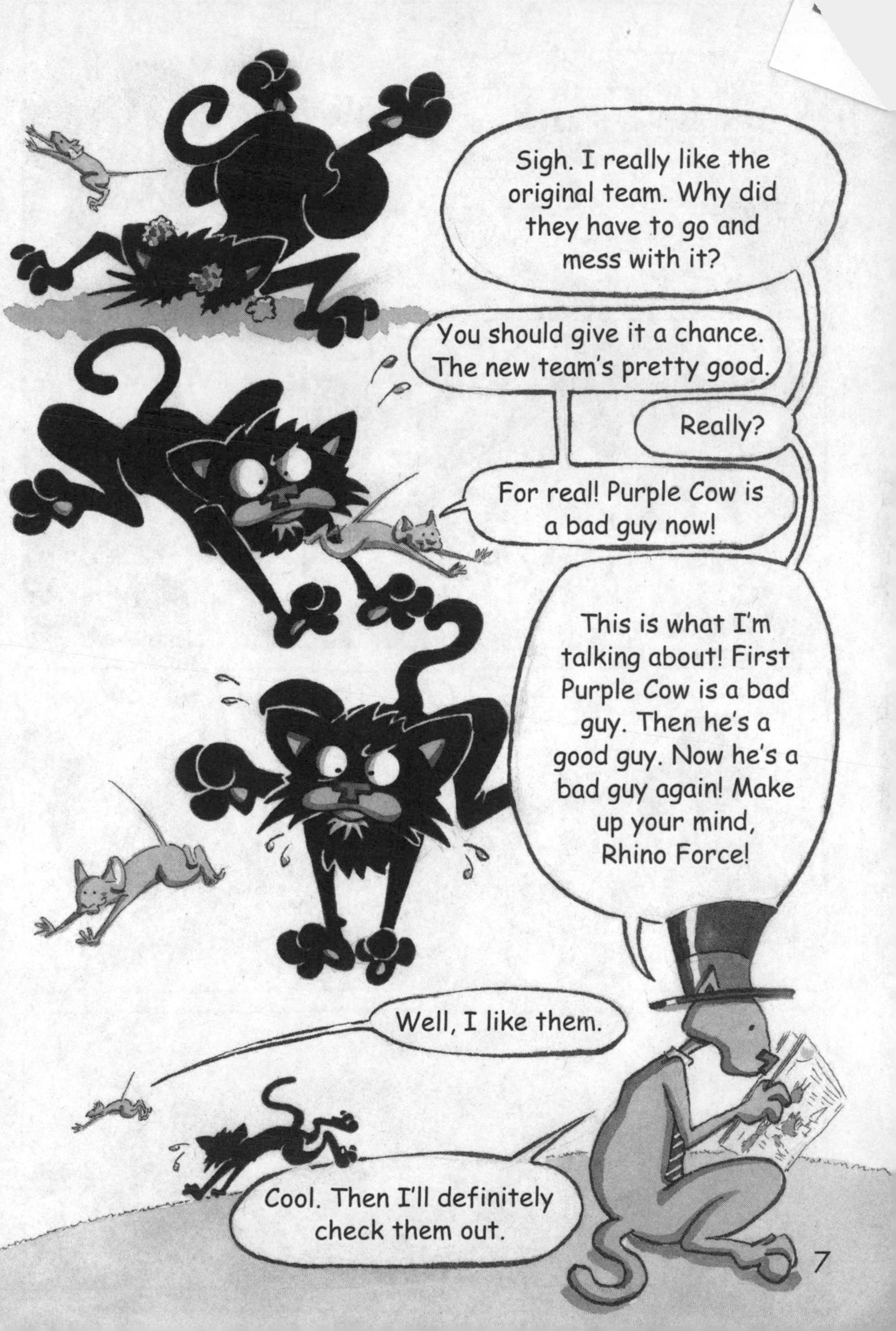
Sigh. I really like the original team. Why did they have to go and mess with it?
You should give it a chance. The new team's pretty good.
Really?
For real! Purple Cow is a bad guy now!
This is what I'm talking about! First Purple Cow is a bad guy. Then he's a good guy. Now he's a bad guy again! Make up your mind, Rhino Force!
Well, I like them.
Cool. Then I'll definitely check them out.

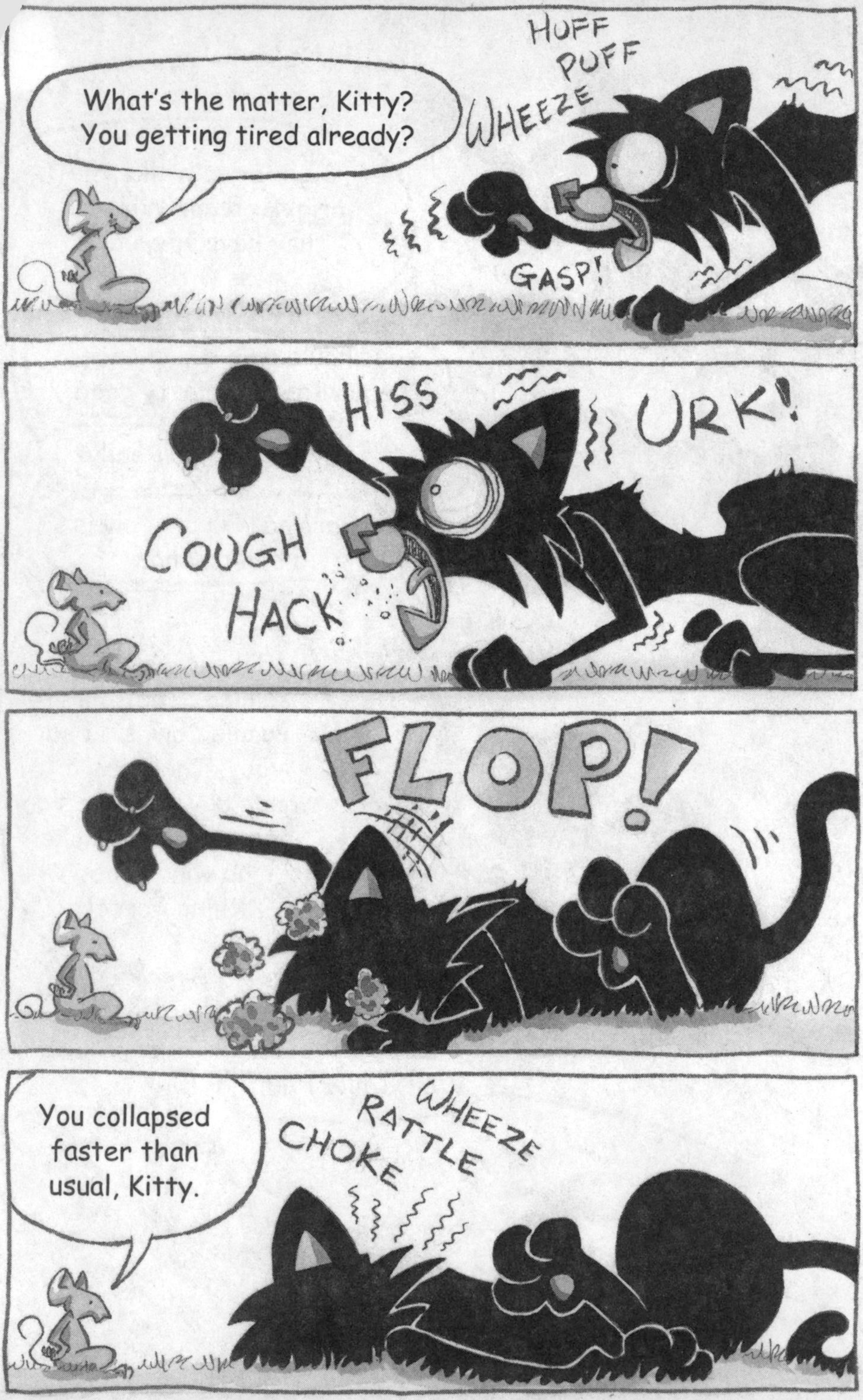
What's the matter, Kitty? You getting tired already?
HUFF
PUFF
WHEEZE
GASP!
HISS
URK!
COUGH
HACK
FLOP!
You collapsed faster than usual, Kitty.
WHEEZE
RATTLE
CHOKE

9

• CHAPTER TWO •

JUST A LITTLE OUT OF SHAPE

Hi, Kitty.

Let me guess—you were chasing Mouse again, weren't you? You'll never catch him. You know that, don't you?

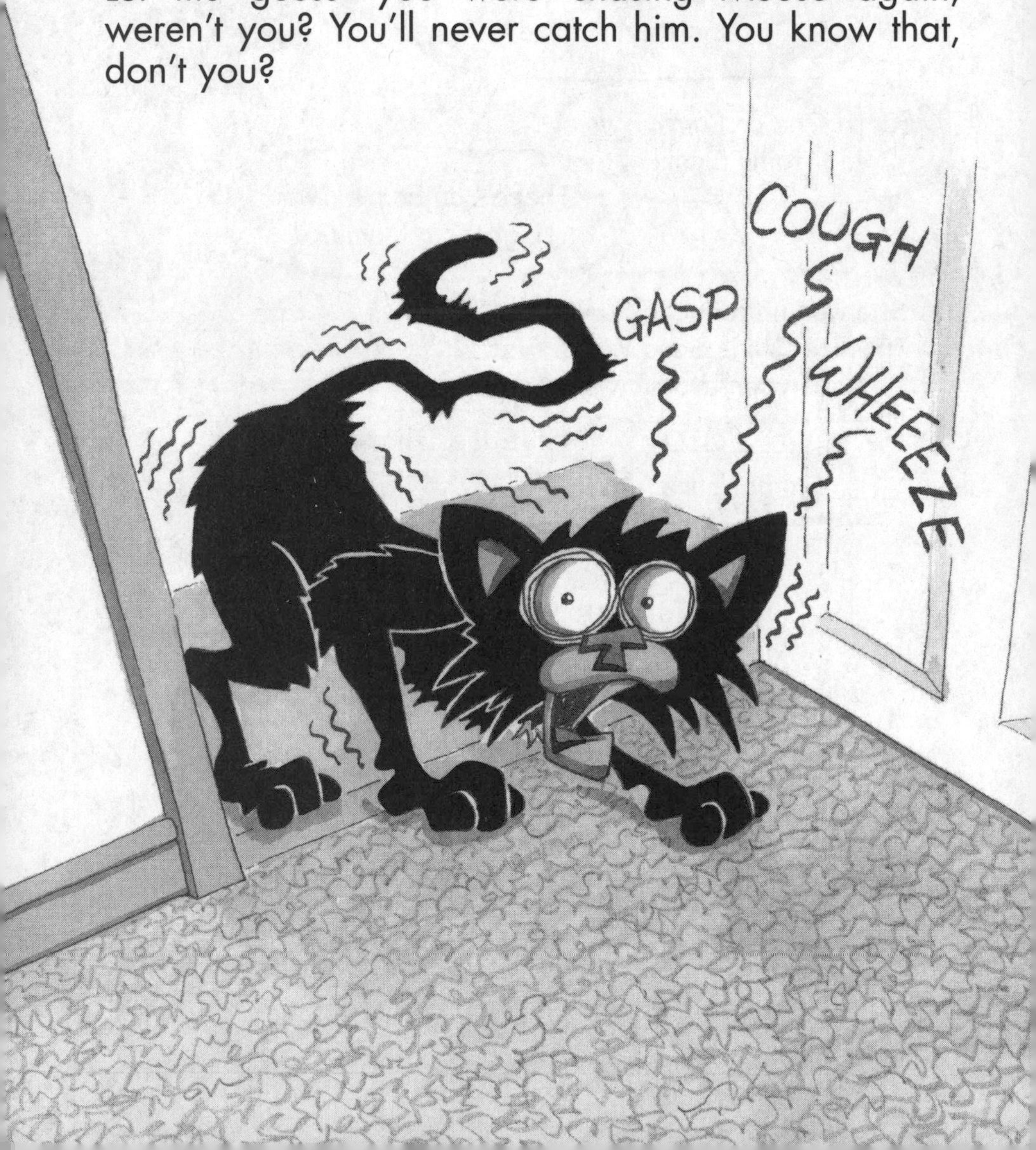
COUGH
GASP
WHEEEZE

KITTY!

Soda is the worst thing for you to drink when you're thirsty! You're dehydrated. Do you know what that means? It means that your body needs WATER.

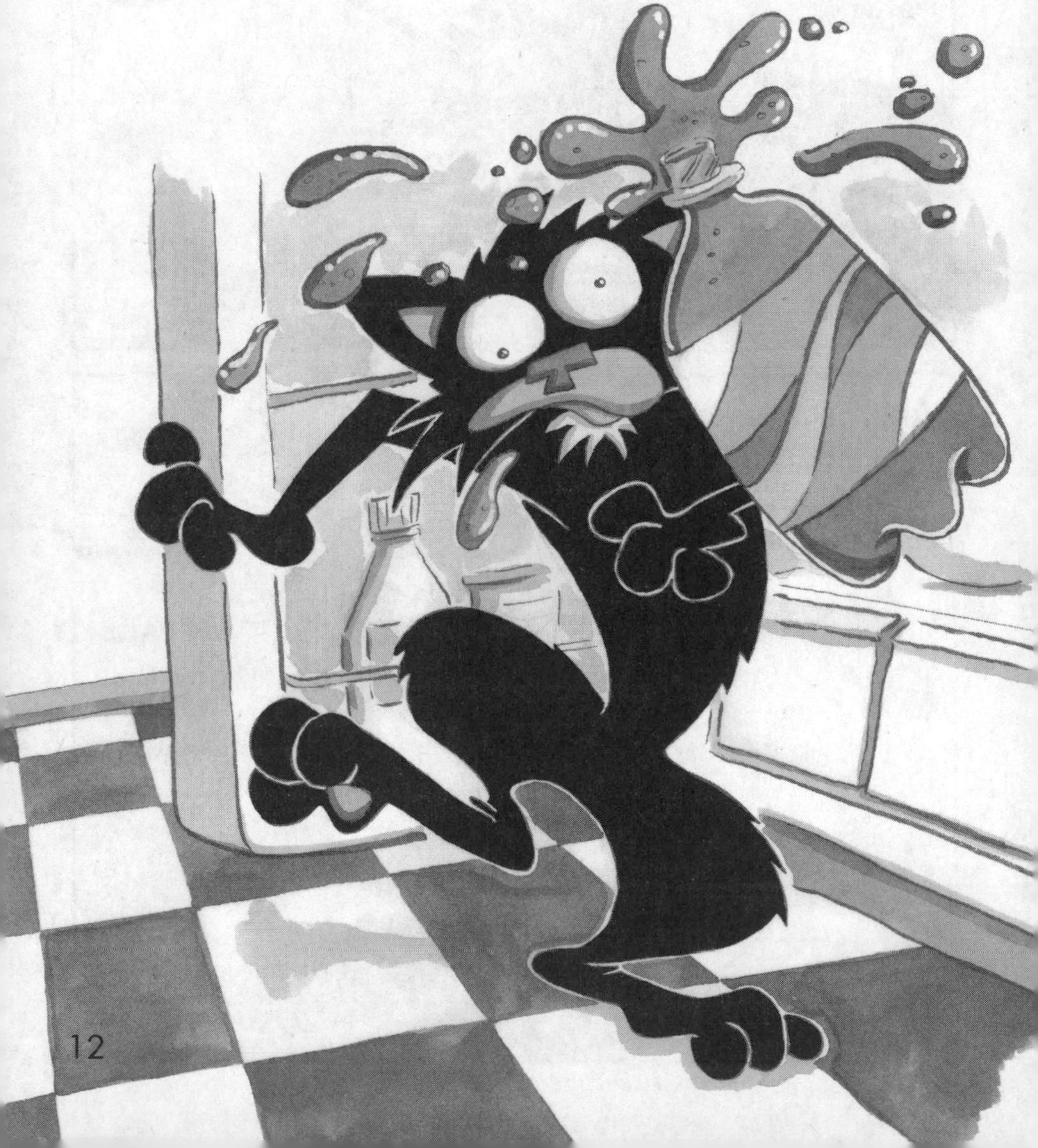

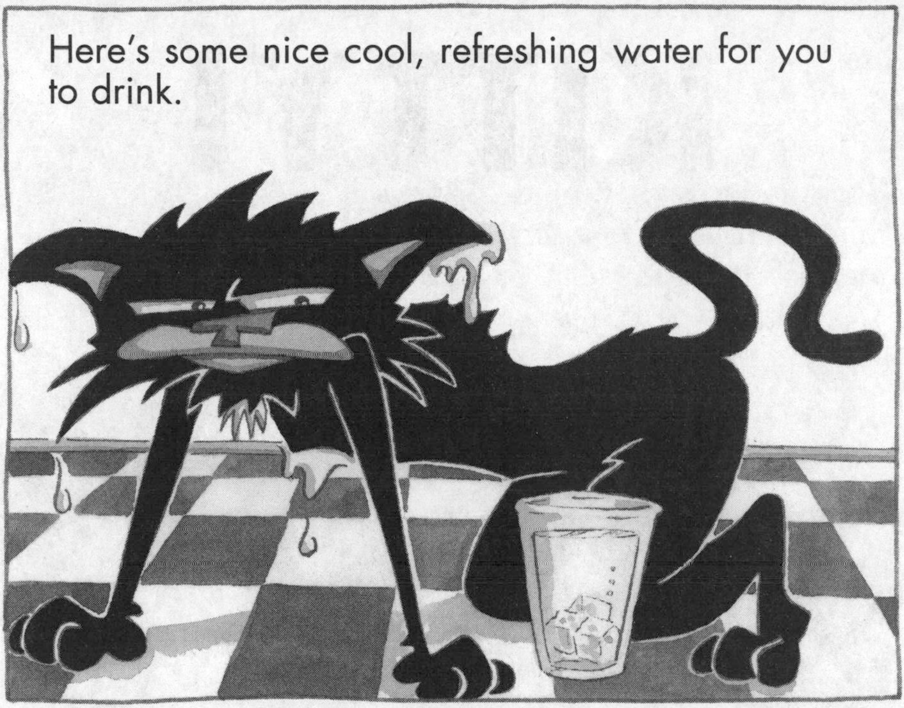
Here's some nice cool, refreshing water for you to drink.

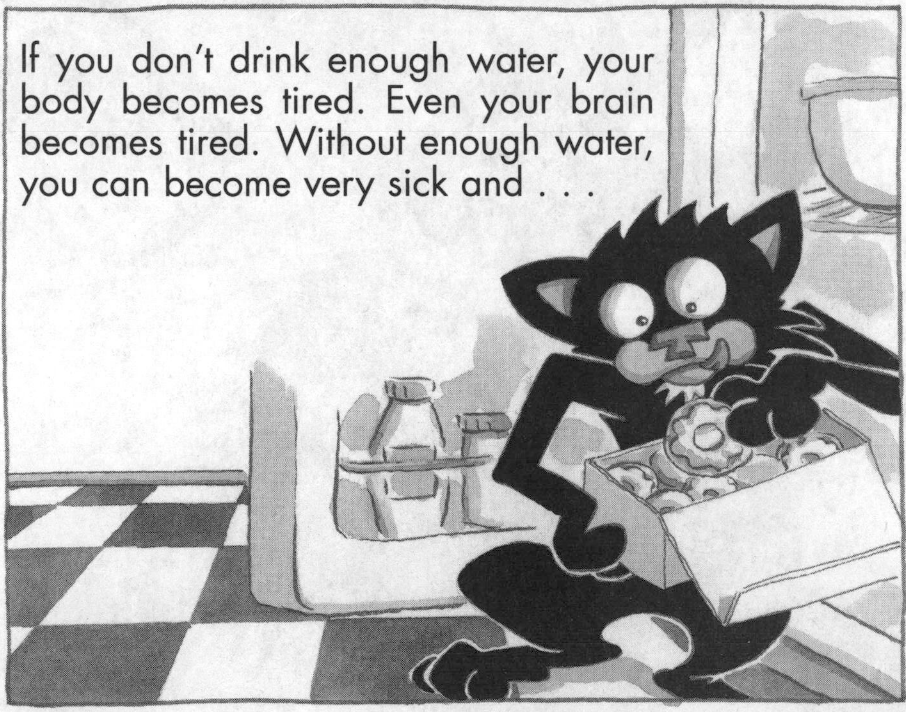
If you don't drink enough water, your body becomes tired. Even your brain becomes tired. Without enough water, you can become very sick and . . .

KITTY!

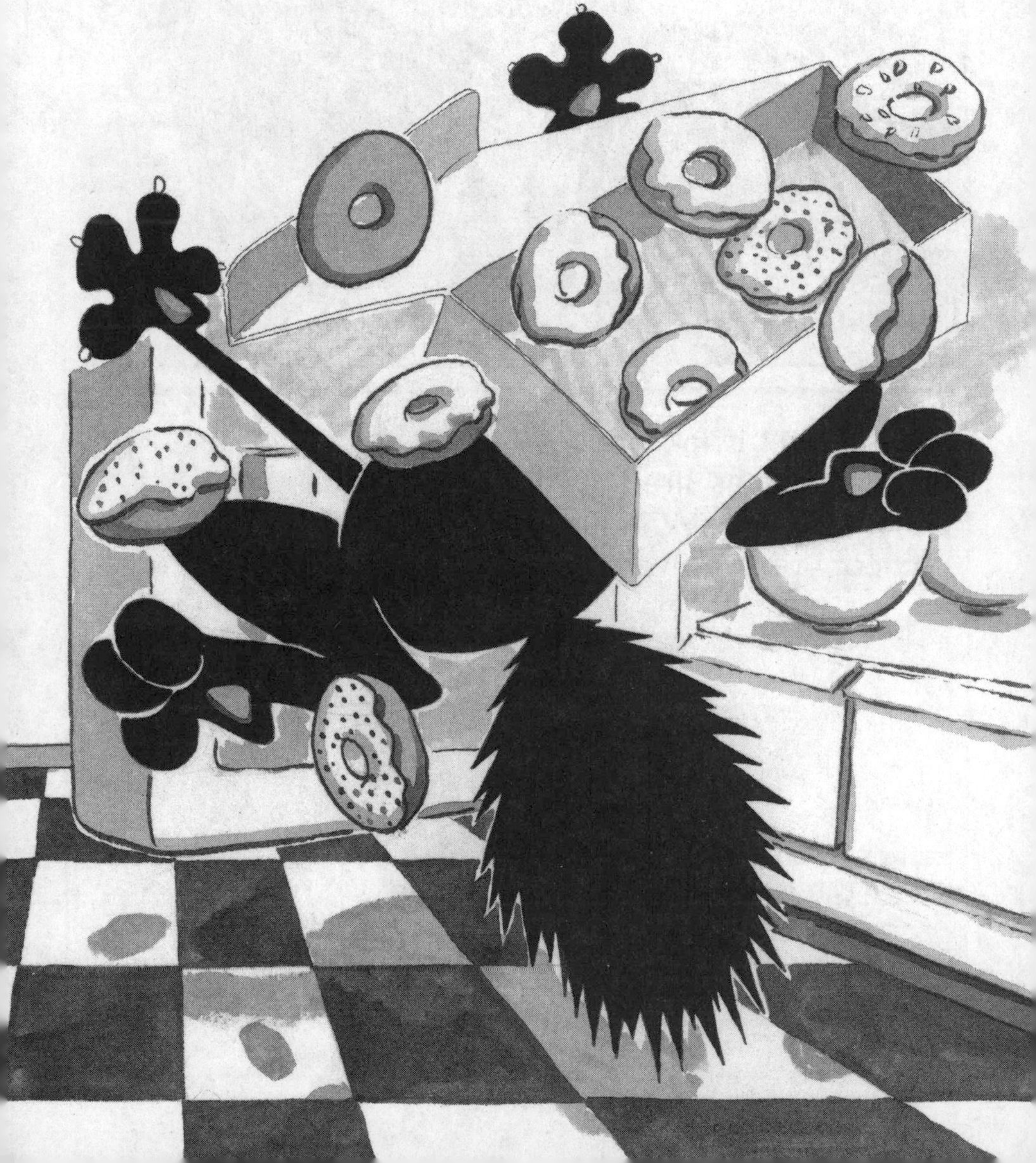

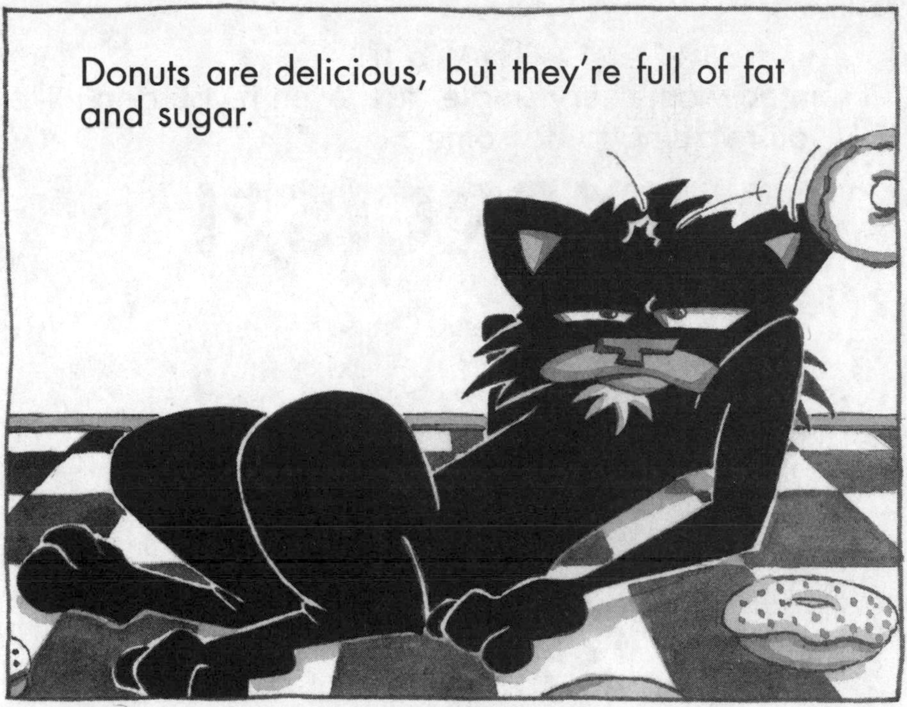
Donuts are delicious, but they're full of fat and sugar.

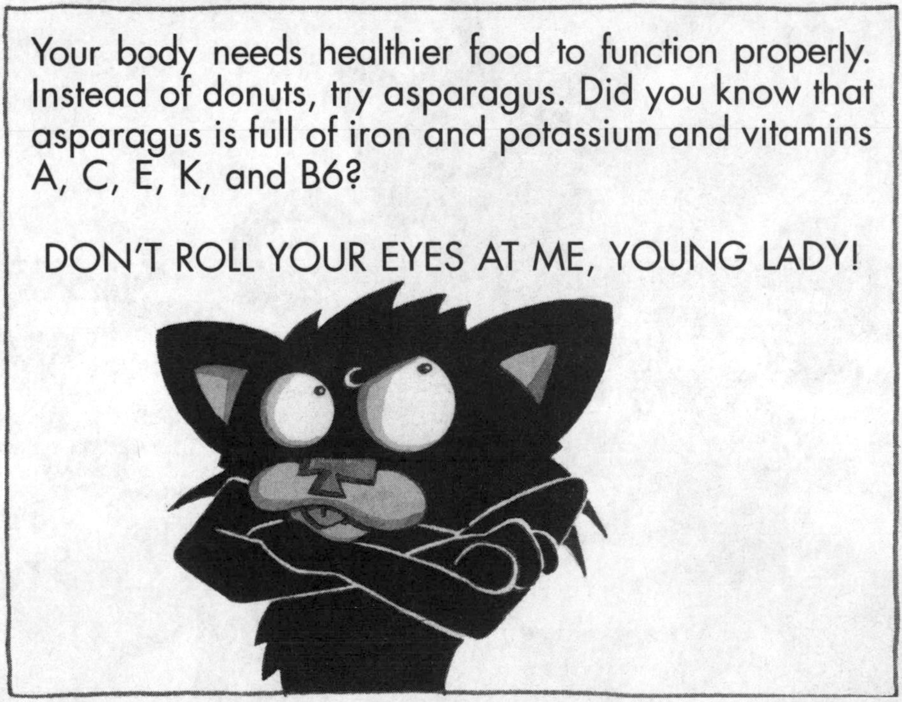
Your body needs healthier food to function properly. Instead of donuts, try asparagus. Did you know that asparagus is full of iron and potassium and vitamins A, C, E, K, and B6?
DON'T ROLL YOUR EYES AT ME, YOUNG LADY!

THAT'S IT!

From now on, every single day, even if you don't like it, you're going to do some . . .

EXERCISE!

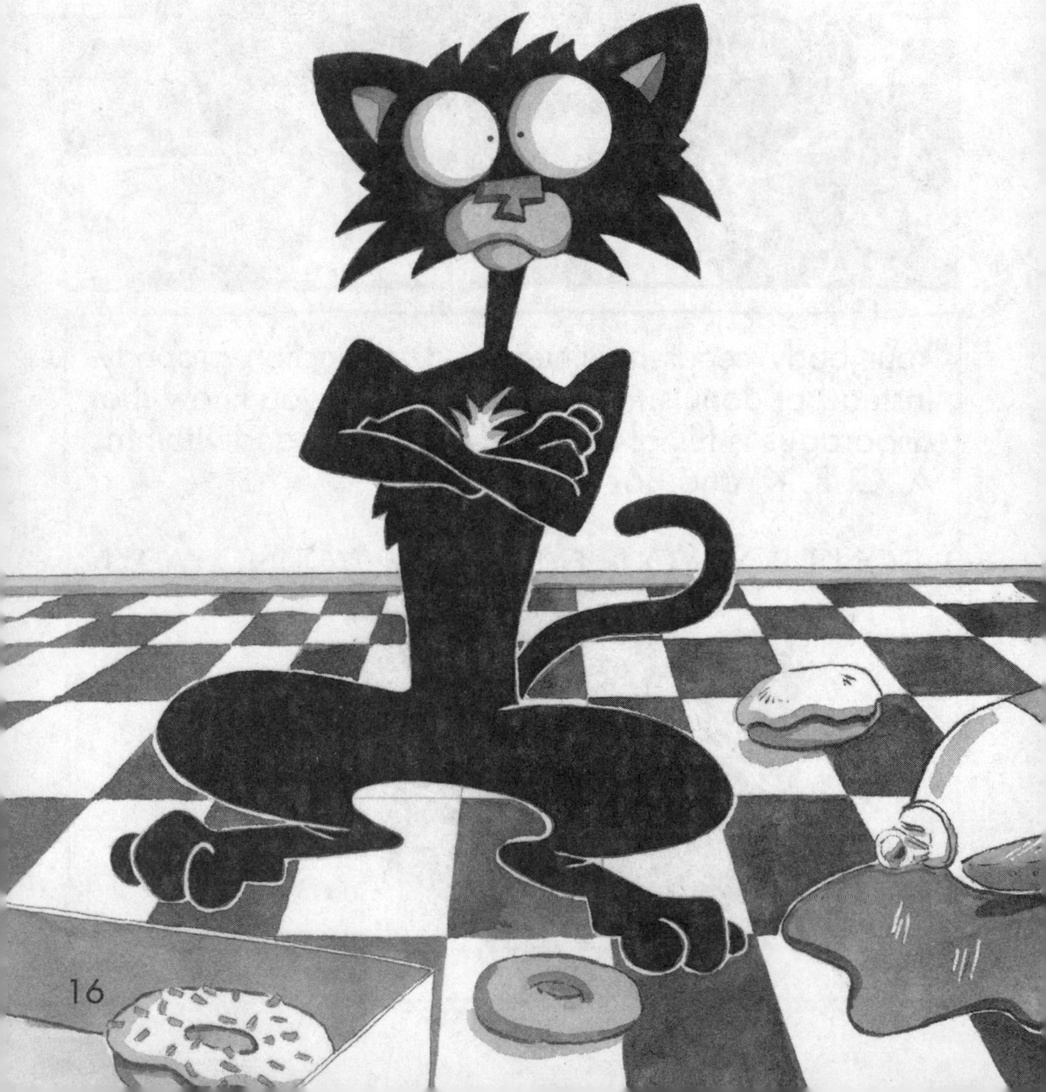

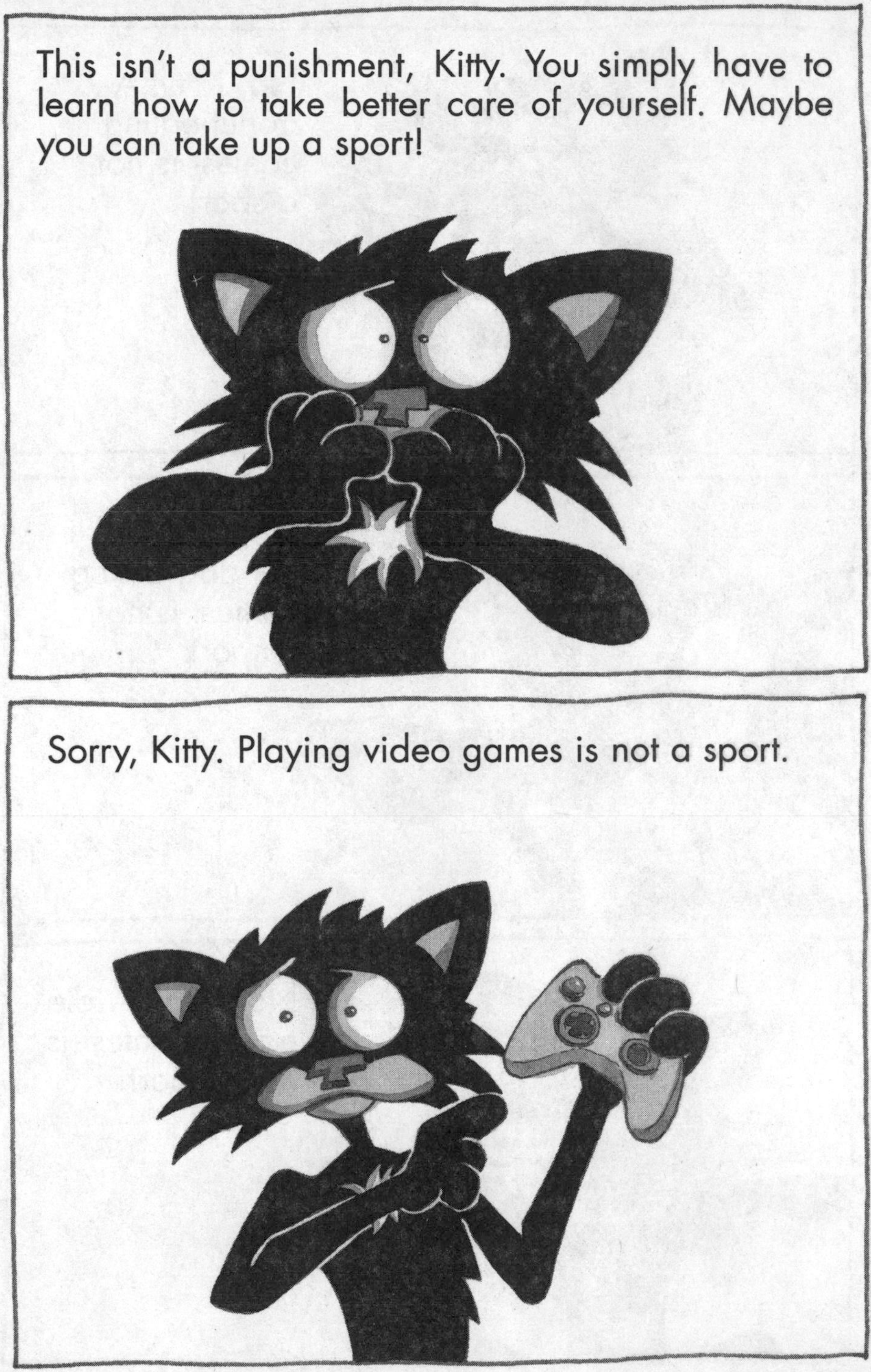
This isn't a punishment, Kitty. You simply have to learn how to take better care of yourself. Maybe you can take up a sport!
Sorry, Kitty. Playing video games is not a sport.

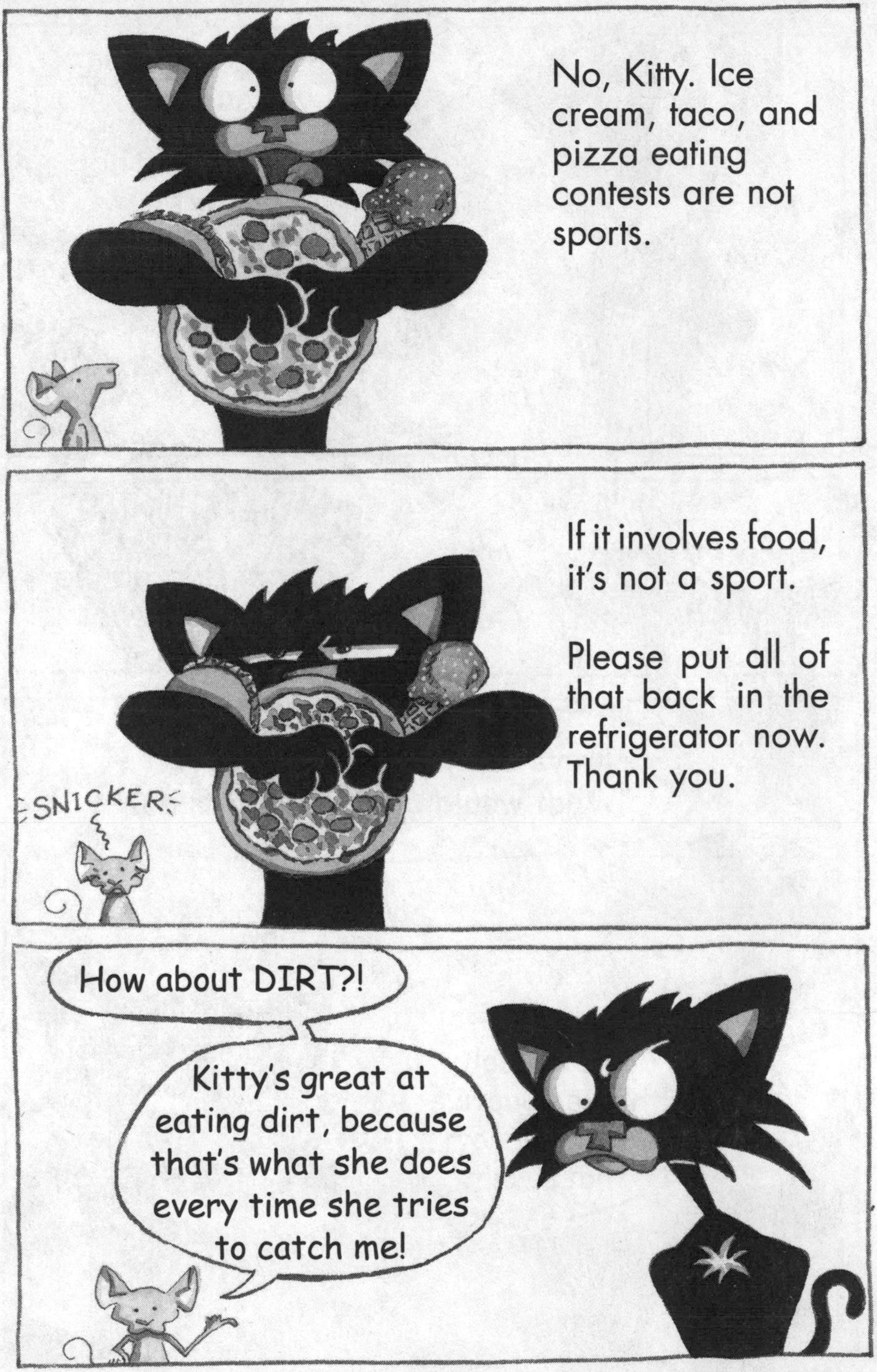
No, Kitty. Ice cream, taco, and pizza eating contests are not sports.
If it involves food, it's not a sport.
Please put all of that back in the refrigerator now. Thank you.
SNICKER
How about DIRT?!
Kitty's great at eating dirt, because that's what she does every time she tries to catch me!

No, Kitty. A mouse-eating contest is not a sport.

Do they even exist?

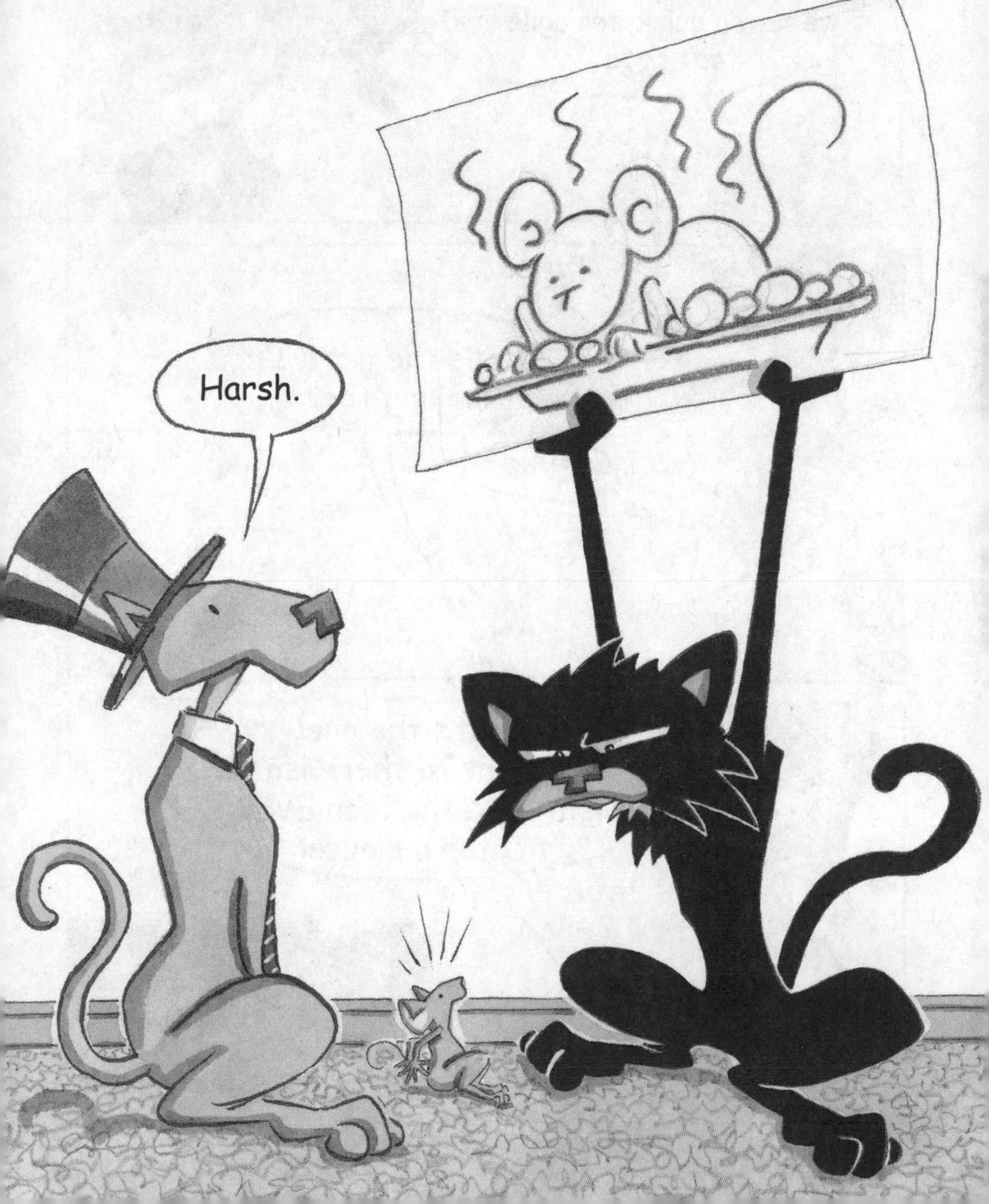
Harsh.

That's right, you maniac!
There's no such thing as a mouse eating contest! Do you know why?! It's because we're too quick, too agile, and too . . . too . . .
What's the word I'm looking for?
Catlike.
That's the one! The point is, there isn't a cat alive that can EVER catch a mouse!

23

STRANGE KITTY'S
UNCLE MURRAY'S FUN FACTS

WHY DO CATS CHASE MICE?

HEY! This is usually MY thing!

Cats are predators. They are born hunters. And one of the animals cats like to hunt the most are MICE.

Unlike people, cats must eat meat to survive. Even dogs can subsist without meat, but not cats. And in the wild, cats find meat by hunting and eating other animals.

Survival in the wild is so important that mother cats will train their kittens to hunt by bringing them live mice on which to practice. The kittens will bat and swat at the mice until they learn the proper way to kill them.

Mice are especially good targets for cats. They're small, they can't fly away, and there are a lot of them.

MICE—
• SMALL
• CAN'T FLY
• LOTS OF THEM
• TASTY

Over many generations, cats have

become extremely skilled at killing mice. Domesticated cats, ones that live with people as pets, kill up to 20.7 BILLION mice and other small animals every year worldwide. These, of course, are cats who have access to the outdoors. If you want to prevent your cat from killing other smaller animals, the solution is simple: Don't allow your cat to go outside. Ever.

Even if a cat is well fed and isn't at all hungry, it will still hunt and kill a mouse if the opportunity arises. It's instinct. It's in their nature to hunt, so they will.

Cats are heartless killing machines! I've been saying this for years now!

Can I have my Fun Facts pages back now?

Kitty!
Did you hear that? These contests are just the sort of thing you need! You'll be able to compete and exercise at the same time!

Kitty?
Where are you?

Kitty?

Kitty?

Oh, Kitty.

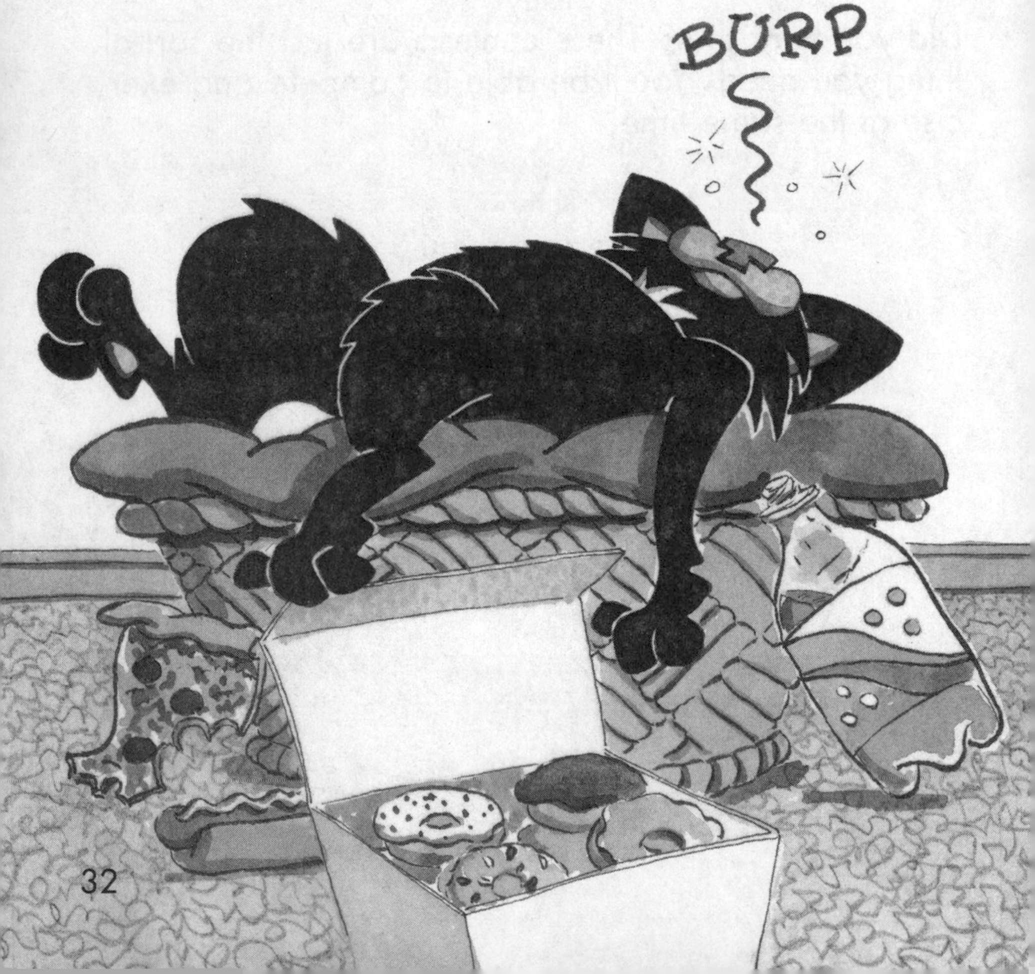
BURP

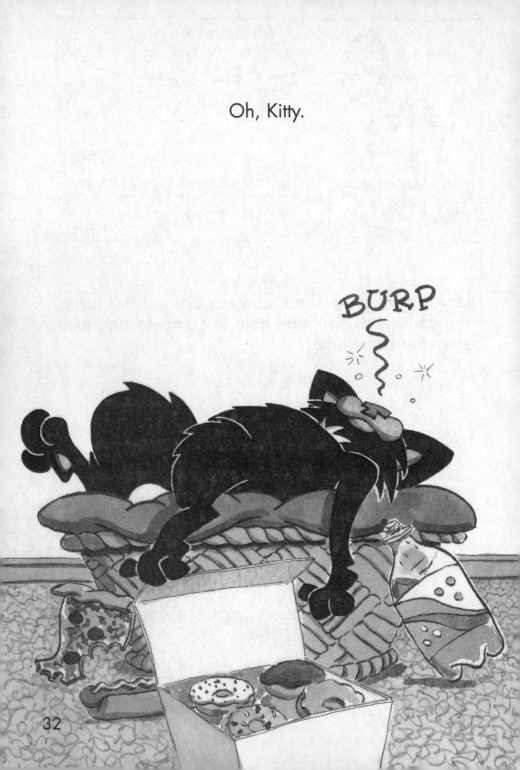

• CHAPTER THREE •

NEGOTIATIONS

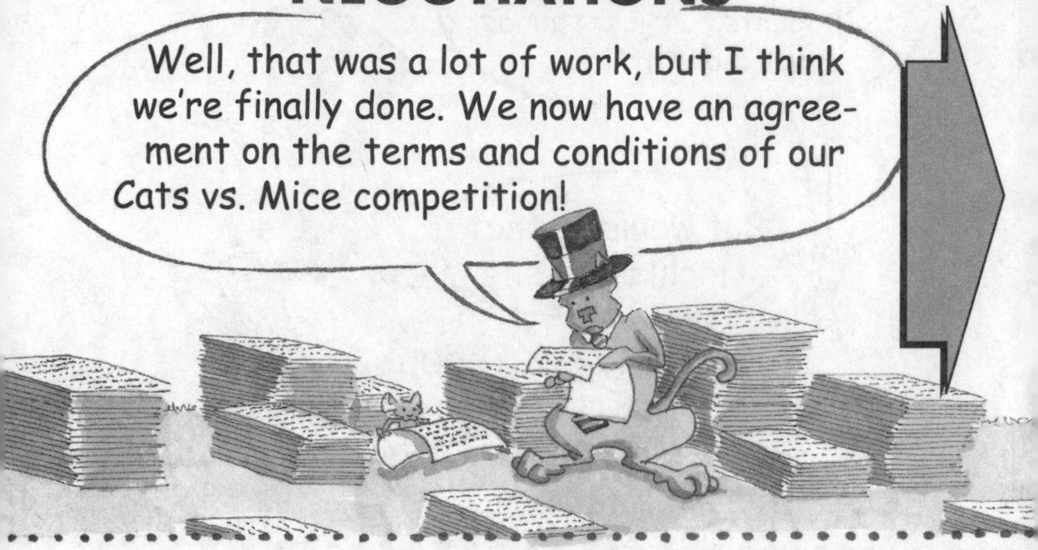
Well, that was a lot of work, but I think we're finally done. We now have an agreement on the terms and conditions of our Cats vs. Mice competition!

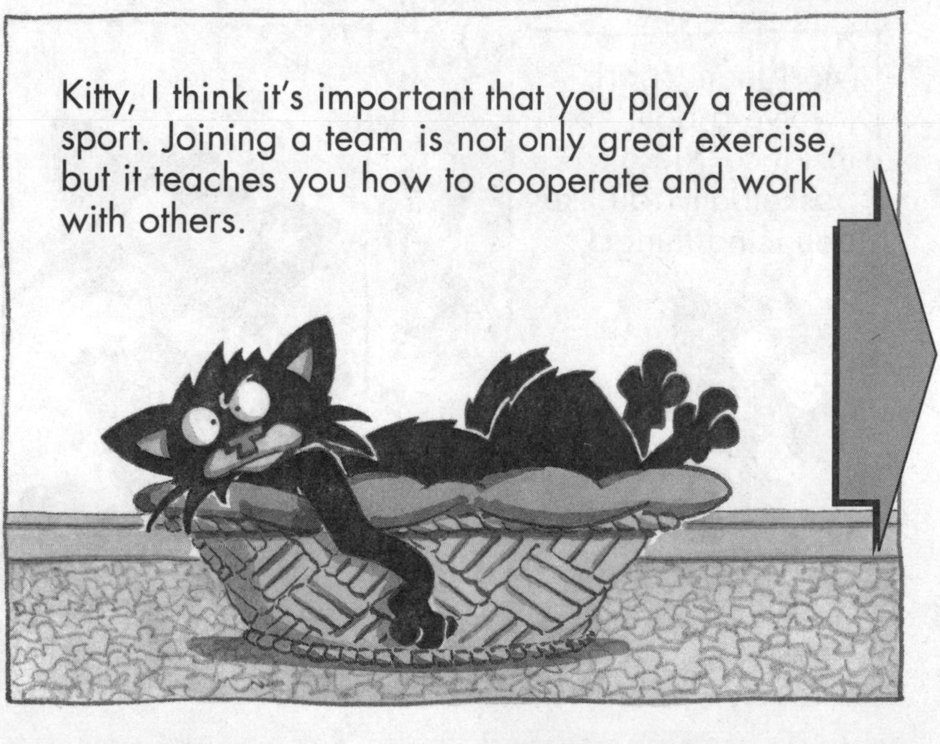
Kitty, I think it's important that you play a team sport. Joining a team is not only great exercise, but it teaches you how to cooperate and work with others.

Hmmm . . . I think I'd like to change the word "Mice" to "Rodents." It just sounds much more official.
But wouldn't that include rats?

Most team sports involve a ball. For instance, there's basketball. You like bouncing things!
POP
FIZZLE
HEH-HEH

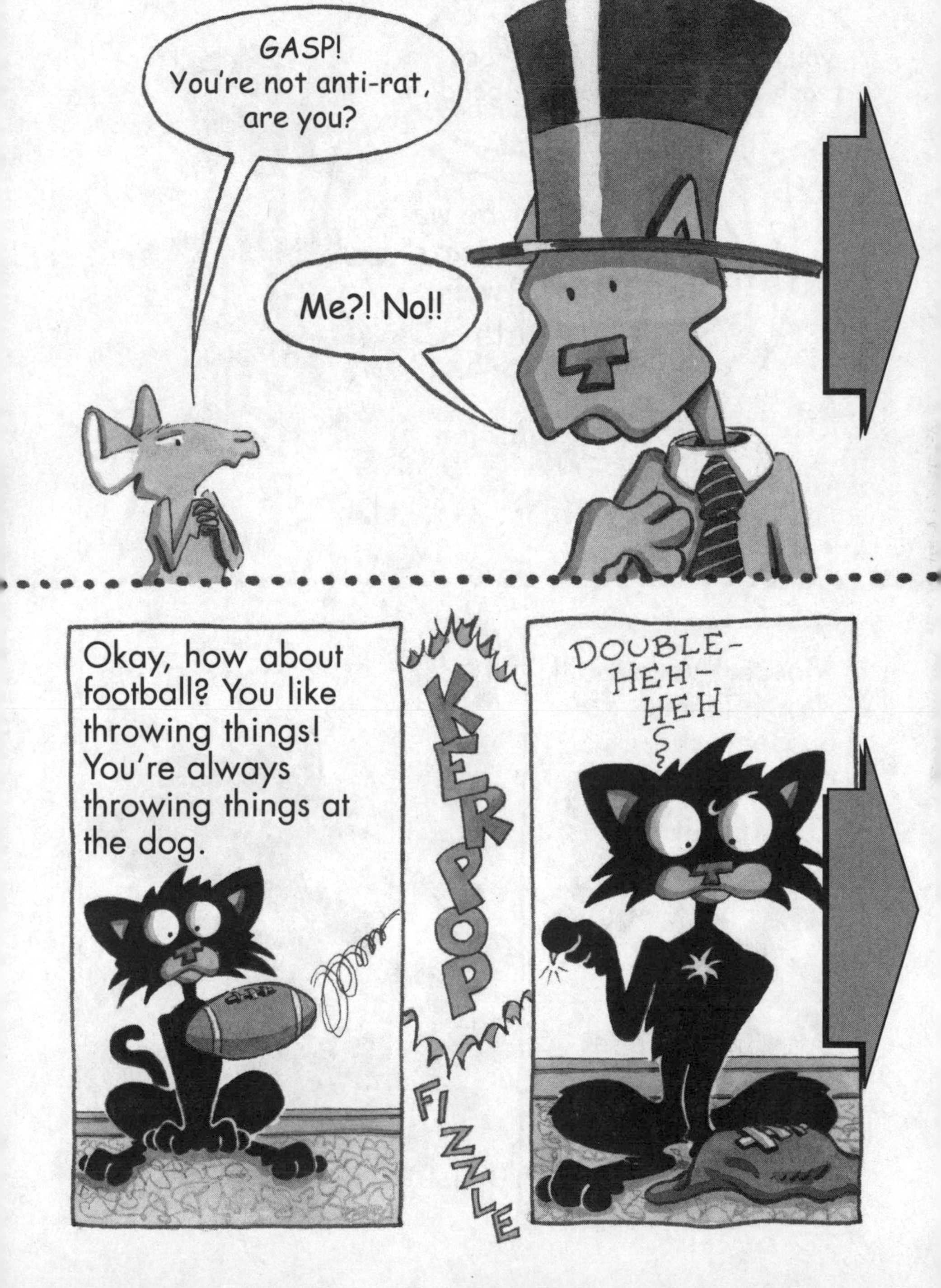
GASP! You're not anti-rat, are you?
Me?! No!!
Okay, how about football? You like throwing things! You're always throwing things at the dog.
KERPOP
FIZZLE
DOUBLE-HEH-HEH

WHOA! WHOA! WHOA! That would include tigers and pumas and all sorts of ferocious beasts! You're not trying to give yourself an unfair advantage, are you?
Of course not! I . . .
Come on, Kitty! Work with me! Let's talk about baseball.
You like hitting things with a bat— unfortunately.
POKE POKE POKE
HMMMMMM...

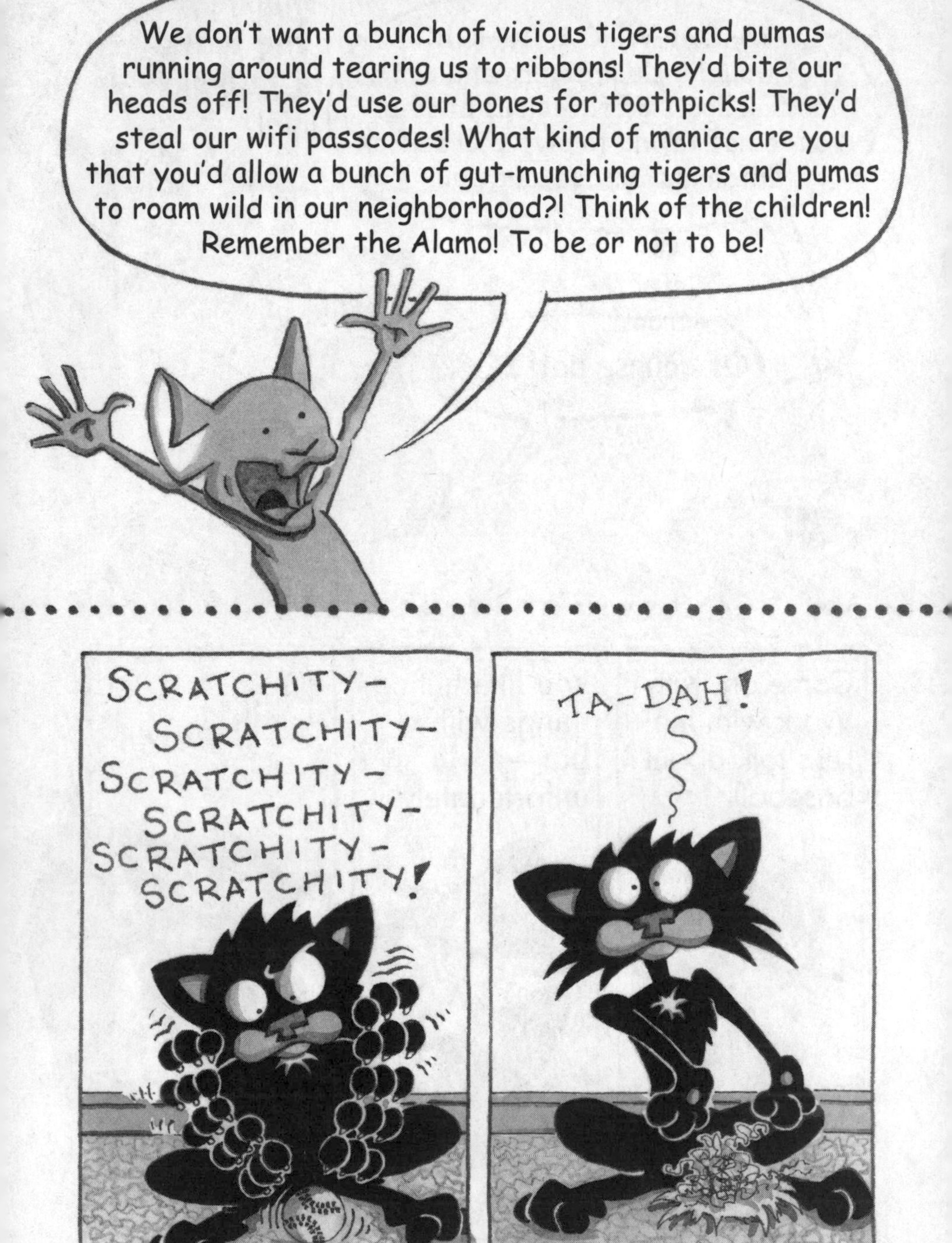
We don't want a bunch of vicious tigers and pumas running around tearing us to ribbons! They'd bite our heads off! They'd use our bones for toothpicks! They'd steal our wifi passcodes! What kind of maniac are you that you'd allow a bunch of gut-munching tigers and pumas to roam wild in our neighborhood?! Think of the children! Remember the Alamo! To be or not to be!
SCRATCHITY-
SCRATCHITY-
SCRATCHITY-
SCRATCHITY-
SCRATCHITY-
SCRATCHITY!
TA-DAH!

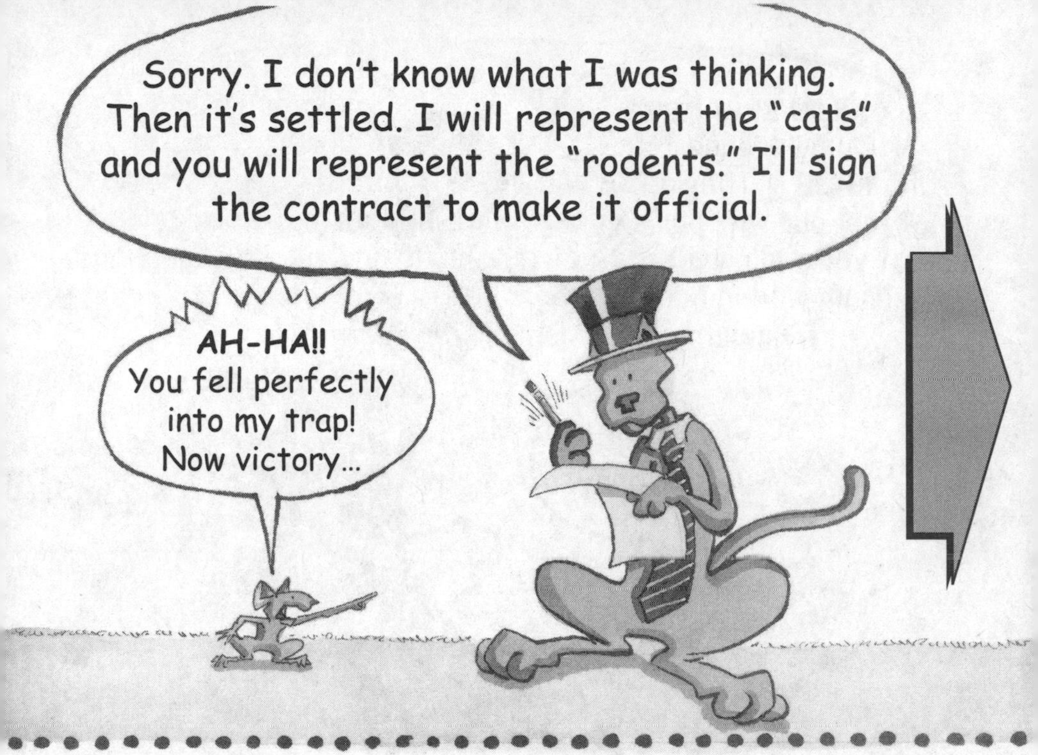
Sorry. I don't know what I was thinking. Then it's settled. I will represent the "cats" and you will represent the "rodents." I'll sign the contract to make it official.
AH-HA!! You fell perfectly into my trap! Now victory...

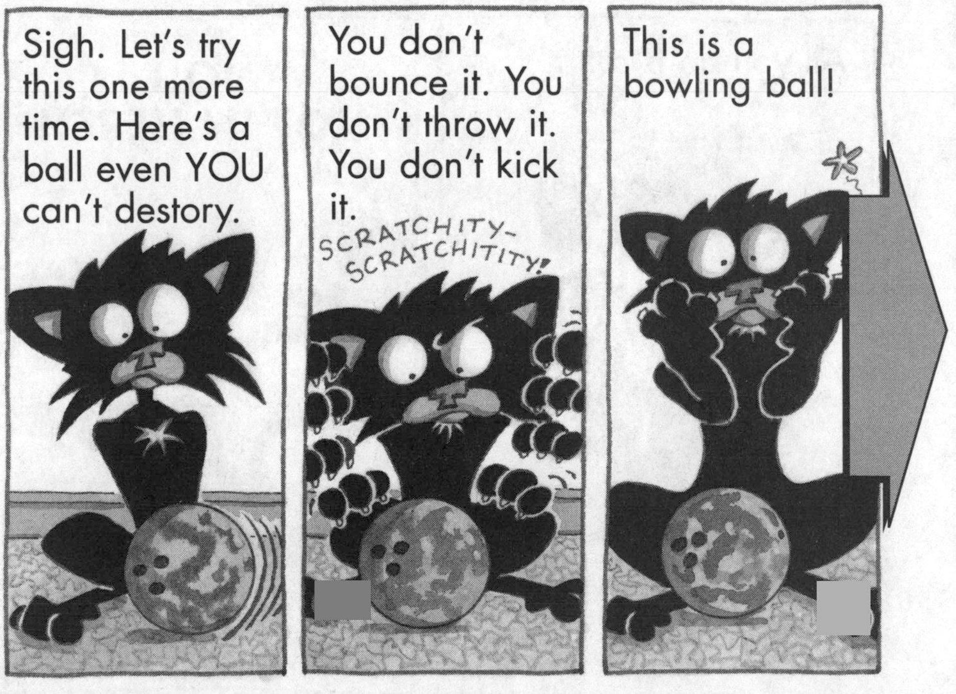
Sigh. Let's try this one more time. Here's a ball even YOU can't destory.
You don't bounce it. You don't throw it. You don't kick it.
SCRATCHITY-SCRATCHITITY!
This is a bowling ball!

THE FIRST EVENT: 100-METER DASH

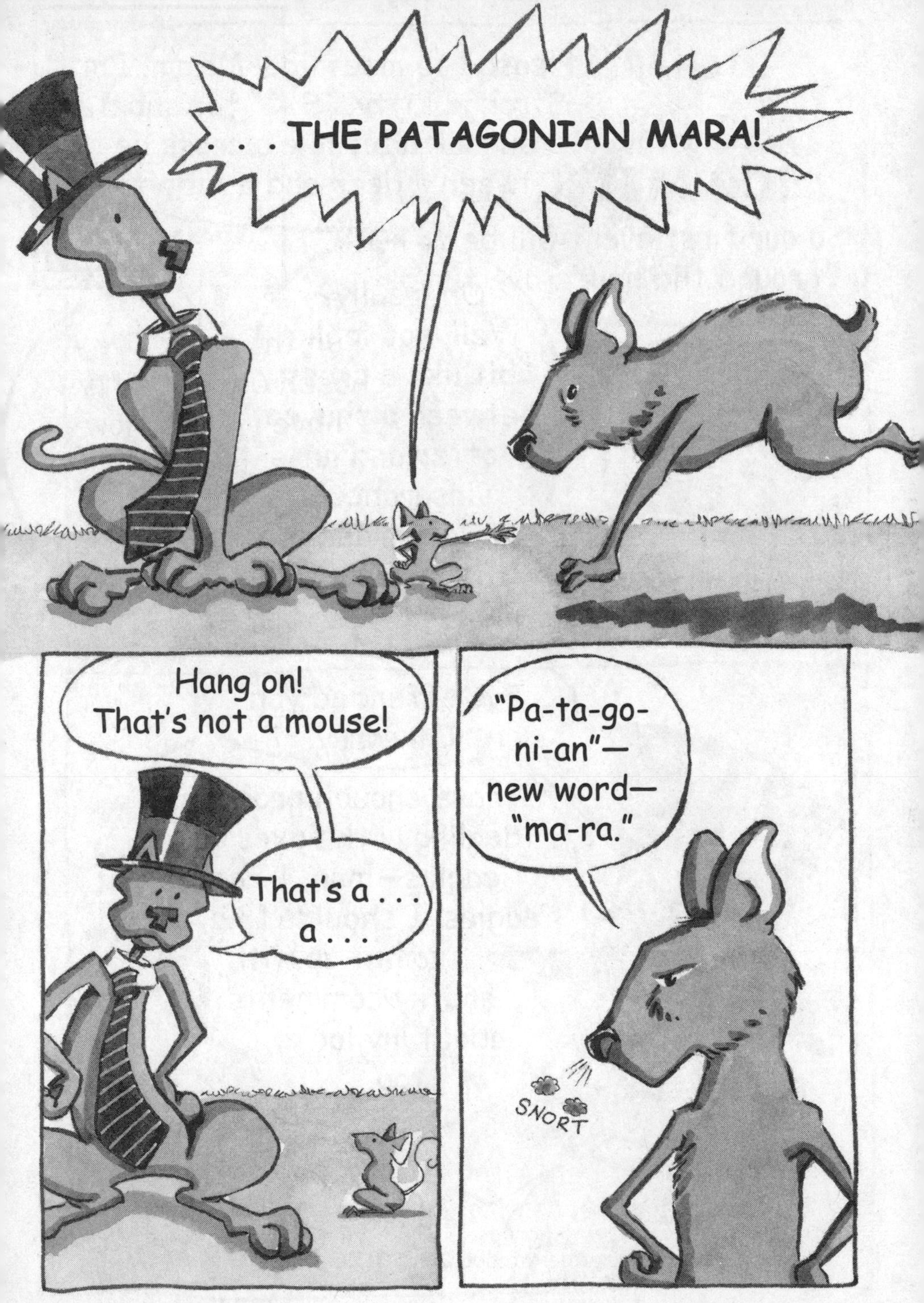
. . . THE PATAGONIAN MARA!
Hang on! That's not a mouse!
That's a . . . a . . .
"Pa-ta-go-ni-an"—new word—"ma-ra."
SNORT

46

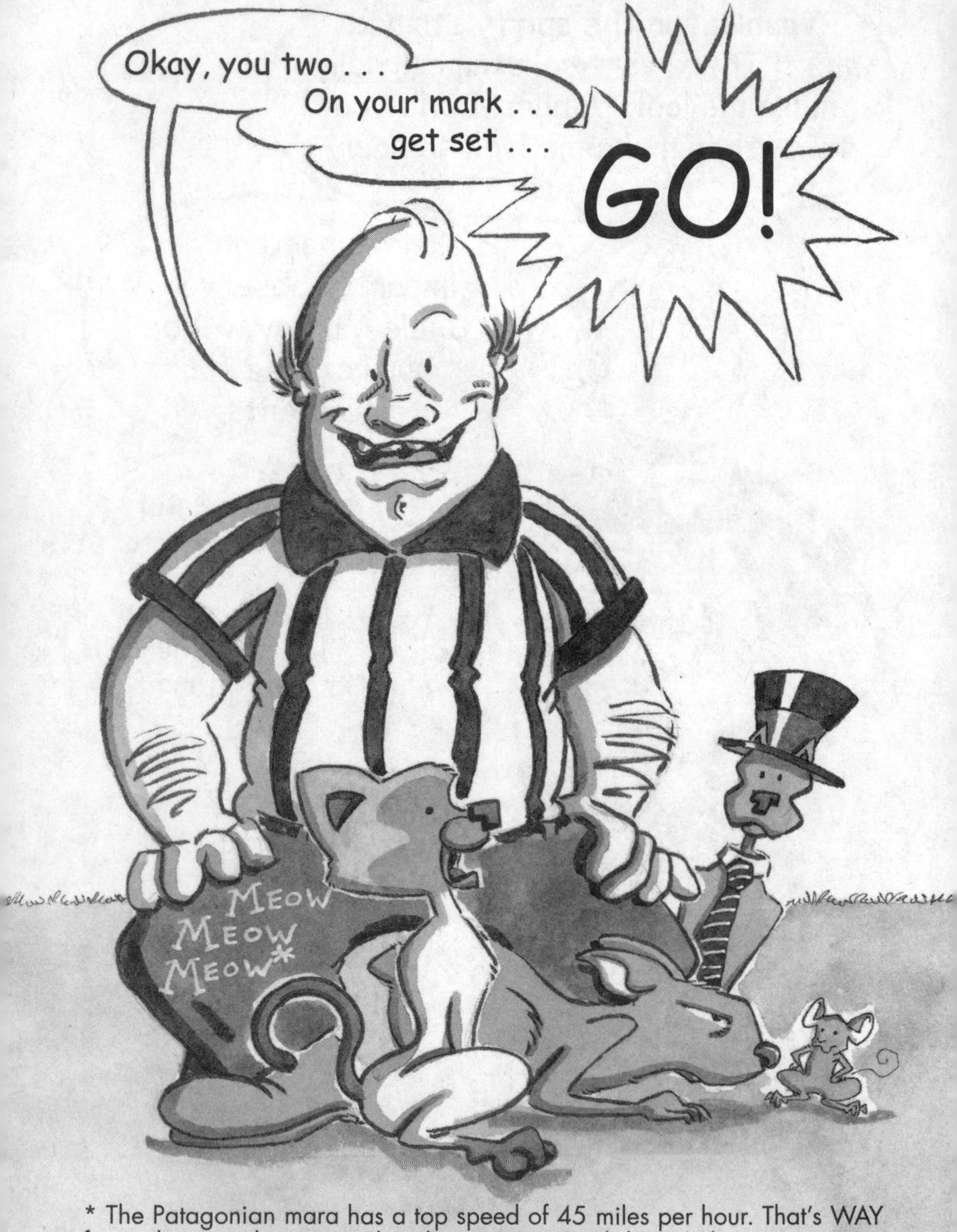
Okay, you two . . .
On your mark . . .
get set . . .
GO!
MEOW
MEOW
MEOW*

* The Patagonian mara has a top speed of 45 miles per hour. That's WAY faster than any housecat. Plus, they can run much longer distances.

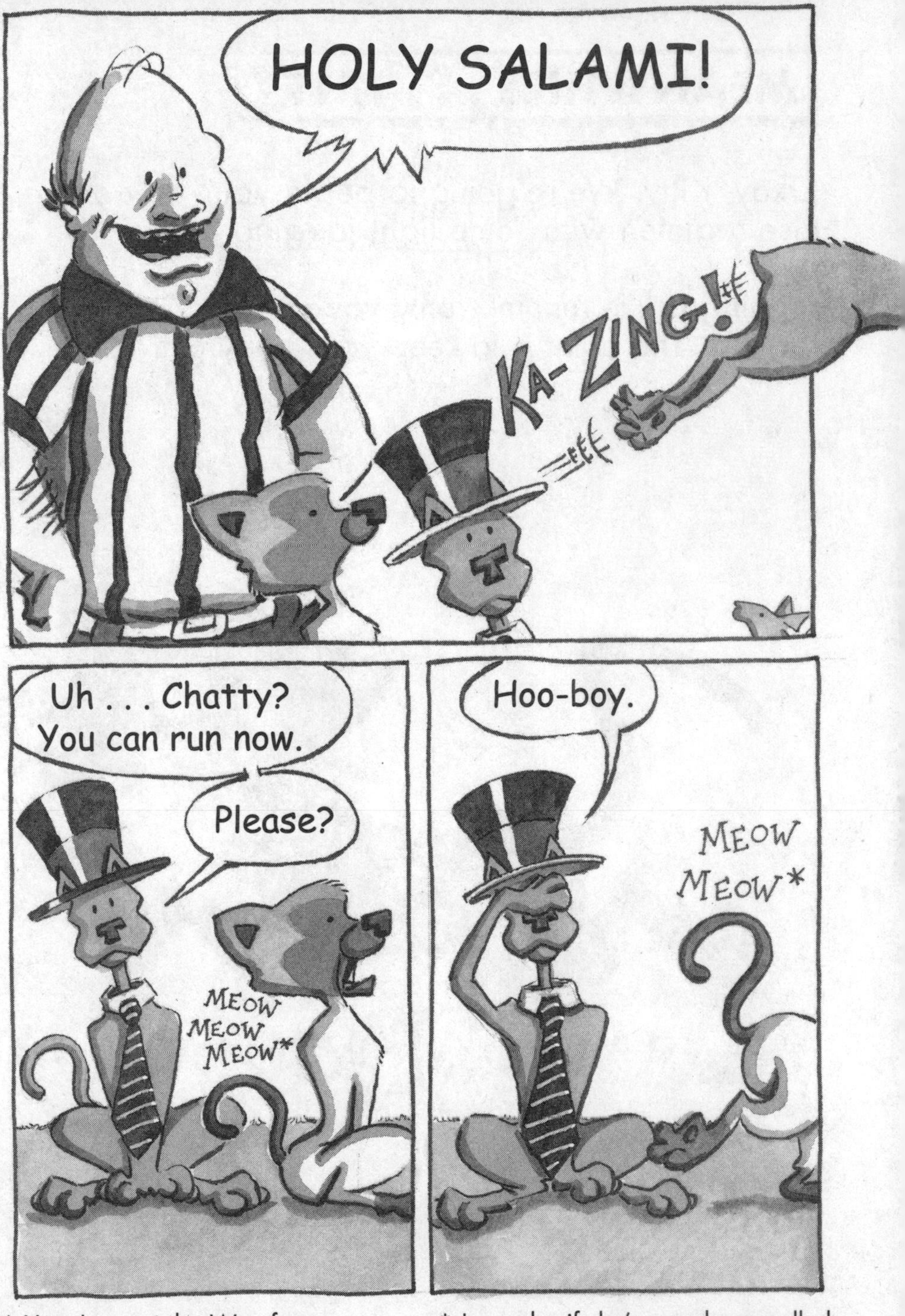
HOLY SALAMI!
KA-ZING!
Uh . . . Chatty? You can run now.
Please?
MEOW MEOW MEOW*
Hoo-boy.
MEOW MEOW*

* Yup. I was right. Way faster.

* I wonder if she's ever been pulled over for speeding in a school zone.

MEANWHILE . . . KITTY

Okay, Kitty. We're going to begin your new exercise regimen with some light jogging.

Jogging is like running, only you're not trying to go too fast. The point is to keep your body active.

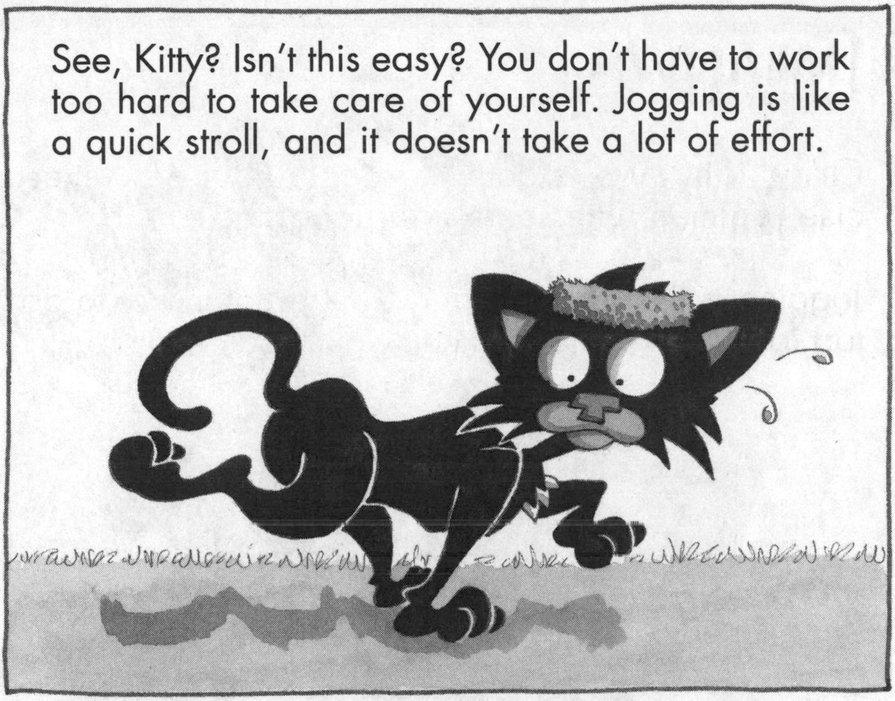
See, Kitty? Isn't this easy? You don't have to work too hard to take care of yourself. Jogging is like a quick stroll, and it doesn't take a lot of effort.

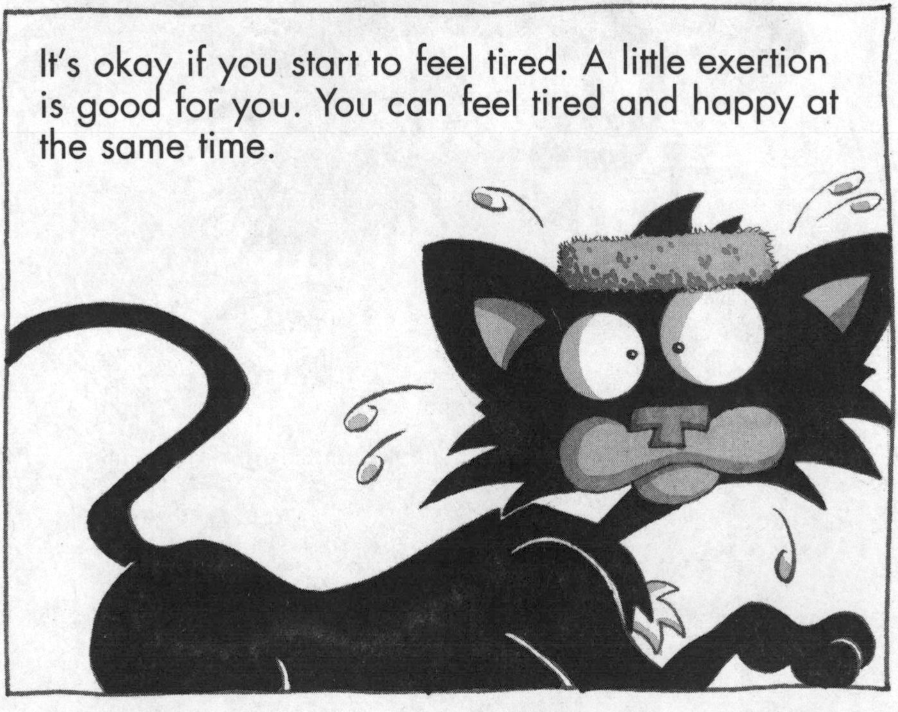
It's okay if you start to feel tired. A little exertion is good for you. You can feel tired and happy at the same time.

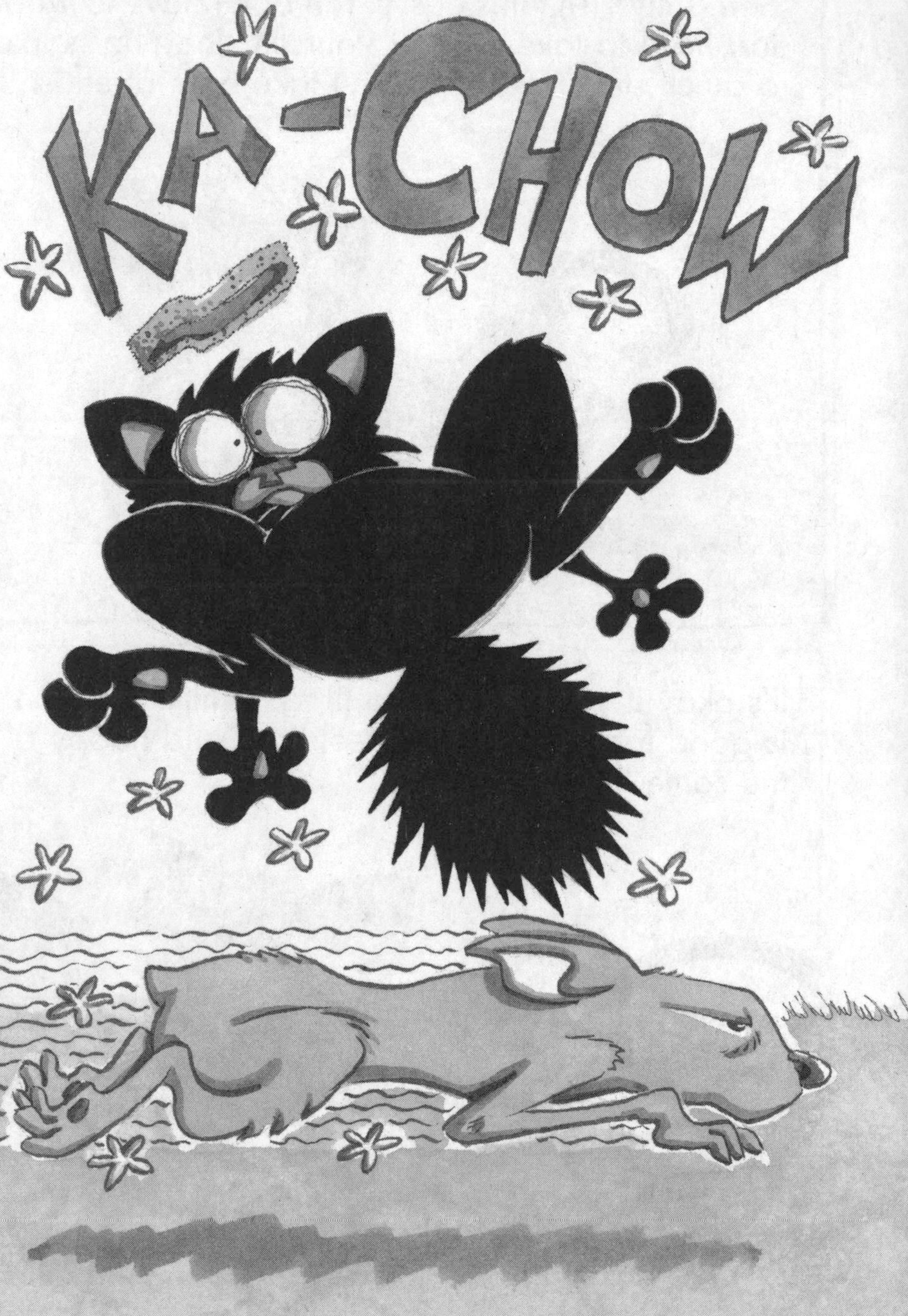
KA-CHOW

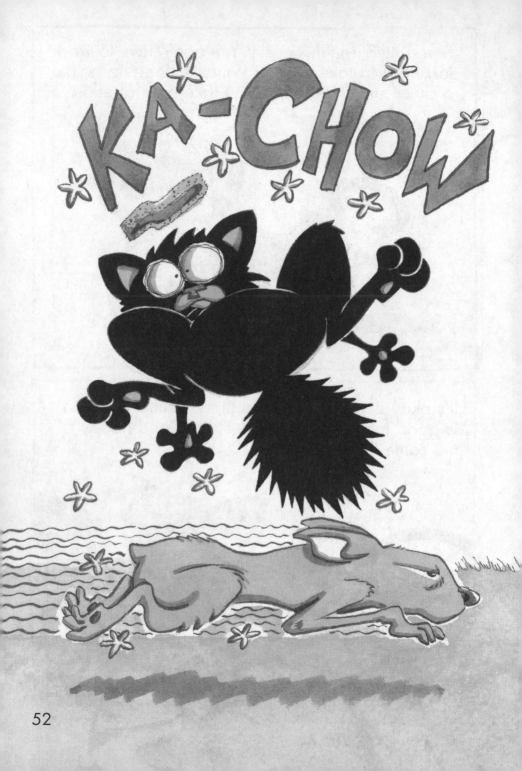

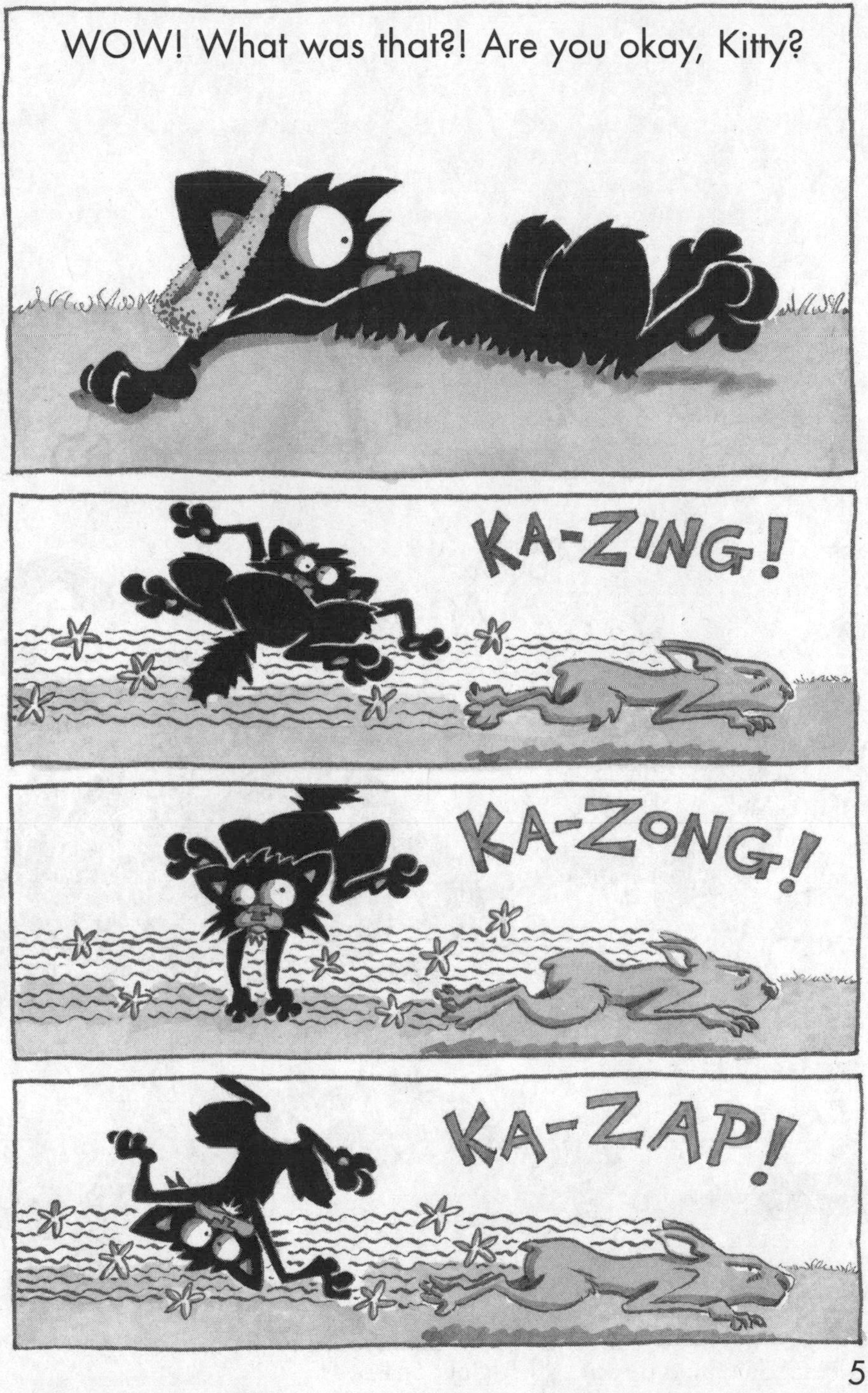
WOW! What was that?! Are you okay, Kitty?
KA-ZING!
KA-ZONG!
KA-ZAP!

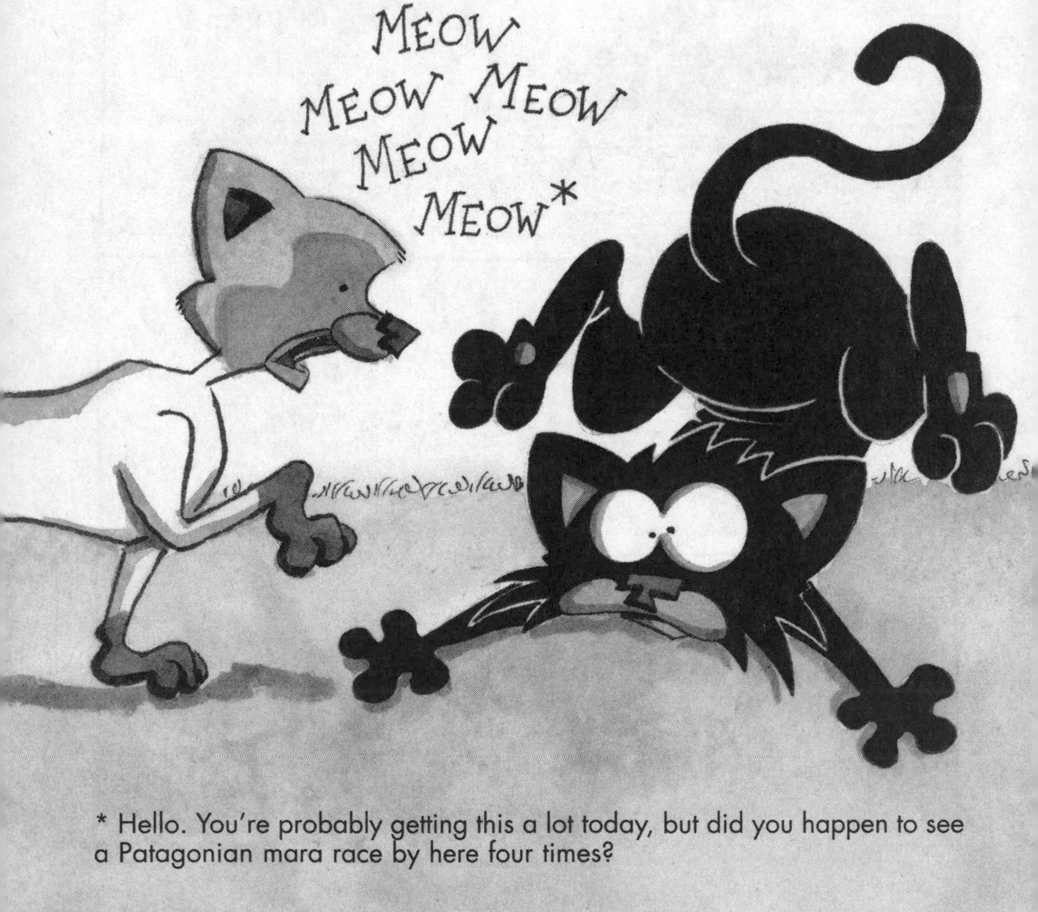
MEOW
MEOW MEOW
MEOW
MEOW*

* Hello. You're probably getting this a lot today, but did you happen to see a Patagonian mara race by here four times?

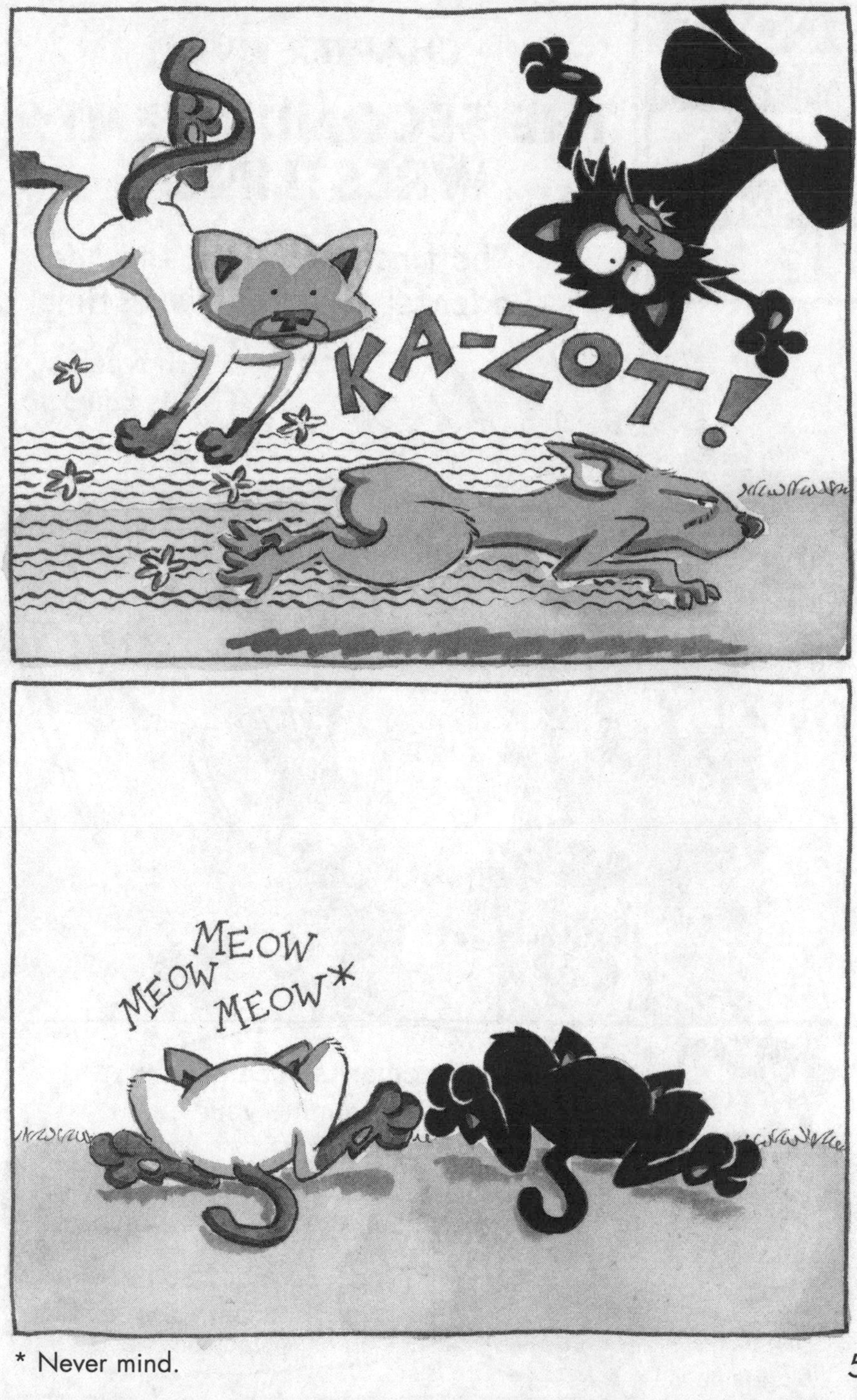
KA-ZOT!
MEOW
MEOW
MEOW*

* Never mind.

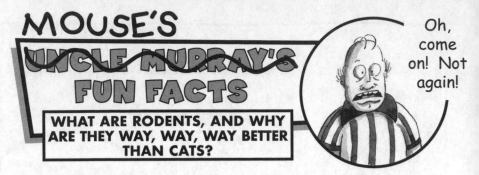

MOUSE'S

UNCLE MURRAY'S FUN FACTS

WHAT ARE RODENTS, AND WHY ARE THEY WAY, WAY, WAY BETTER THAN CATS?

Oh, come on! Not again!

Forty percent of all mammal species in the world are rodents! We come in many shapes and sizes, but the thing all rodents have in common are two pairs of incisors (sharp powerful teeth), one pair on the upper front of our jaw and one pair on the bottom, that never stop growing!

The biggest rodent is the capybara. They look a little like gigantic guinea pigs and can weigh as much as 200 pounds! That's over four times the weight of even the biggest housecat.

CAPYBARA

The smallest rodent is the dwarf three-toed jerboa. Its body length is only about 1.7 inches, and it weighs less than an ounce. No housecat is that small.

DWARF JERBOA

(ACTUAL SIZE)

Some rodents can FLY! There are 43 species of flying squirrels, and each of them can leap from a tree branch, glide as much as 660 feet through the air, and land effortlessly on another branch. If you dropped a cat from the top of a tall tree, it would fall like a bag of wet bananas until it hit the ground with a dull *thud*.

Some rodents practically live in WATER! Beavers, for instance, can hold their breath underwater for 15 minutes! A colony of beavers can build a dam that will block an entire river. Do you know what happens when you get a cat even slightly wet? One little drop of water, and they go insane. Pathetic!

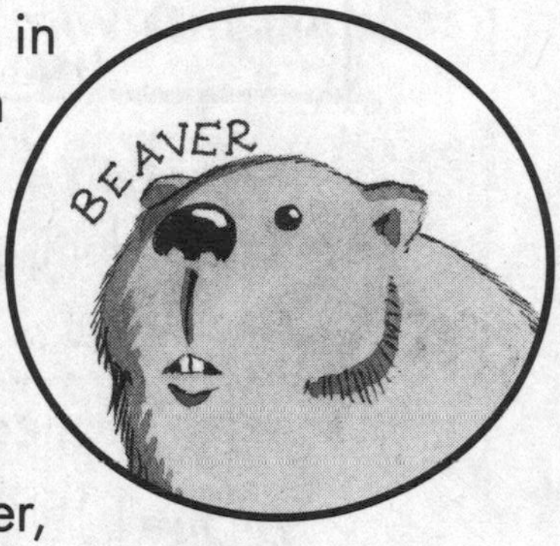
BEAVER

Some rodents live UNDERGROUND! Groundhogs build burrows that can be as long as 60 feet with several chambers, or rooms. They'll even build a special chamber where they can poop. That's right—groundhogs build bathrooms! Cats will do their business wherever there's a patch of sand or dirt. They don't care!

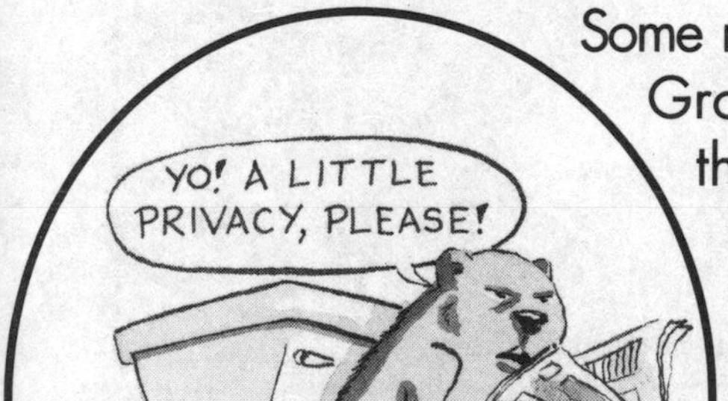
YO! A LITTLE PRIVACY, PLEASE!

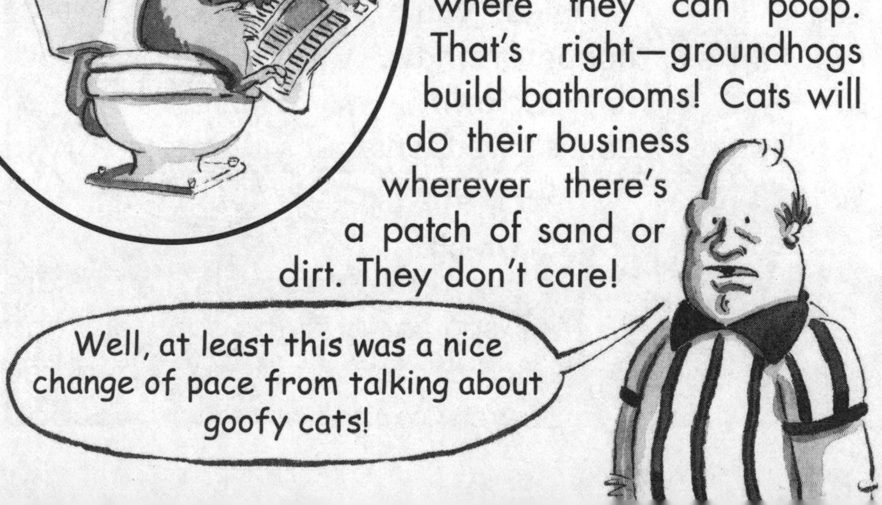
Well, at least this was a nice change of pace from talking about goofy cats!

61

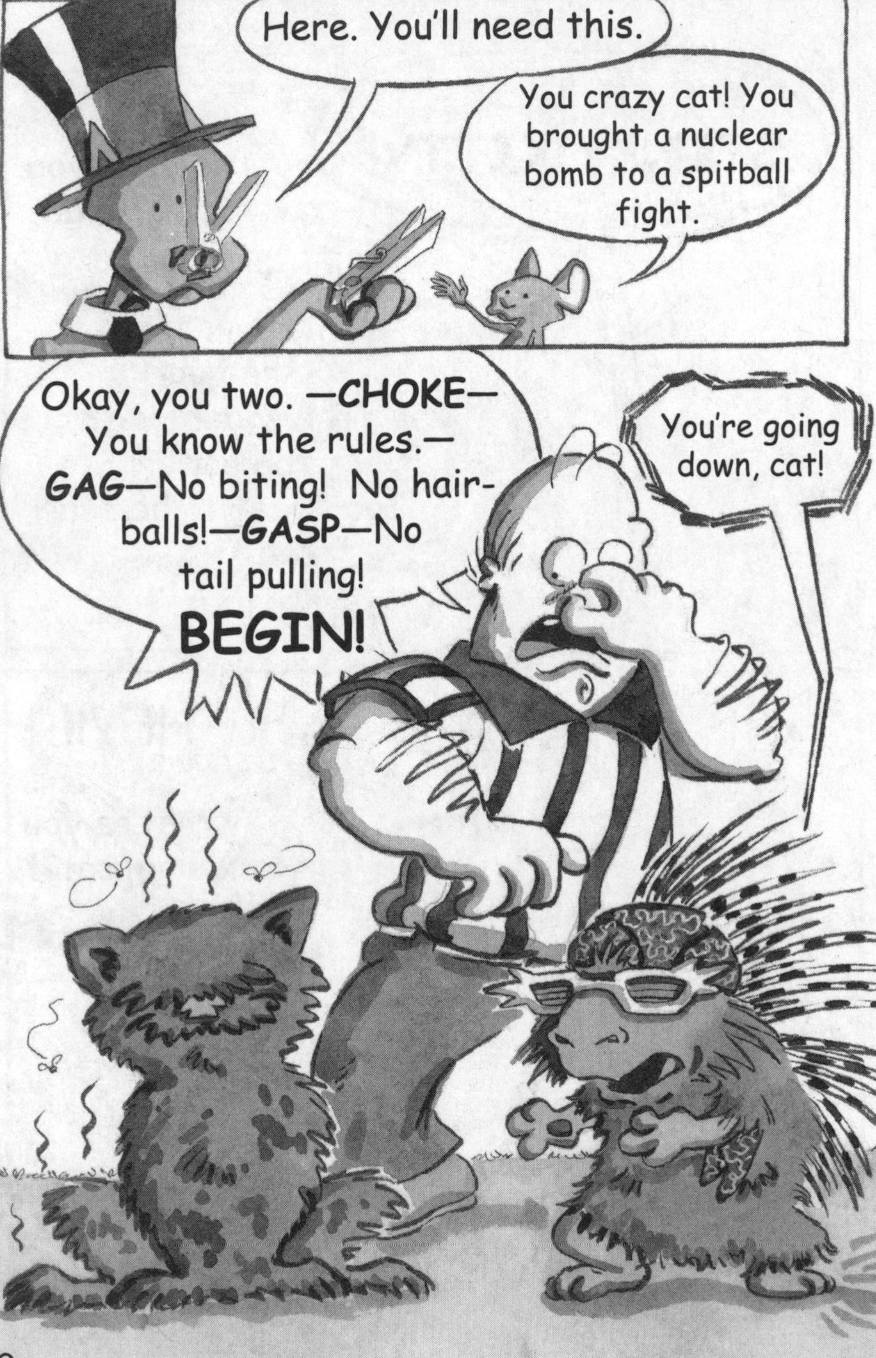

Here. You'll need this.
You crazy cat! You brought a nuclear bomb to a spitball fight.
Okay, you two. —**CHOKE**— You know the rules.— **GAG**—No biting! No hair-balls!—**GASP**—No tail pulling! **BEGIN!**
You're going down, cat!

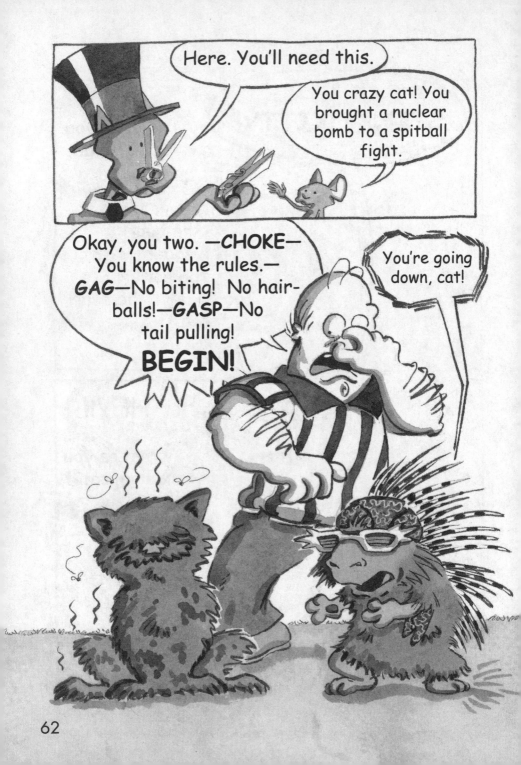

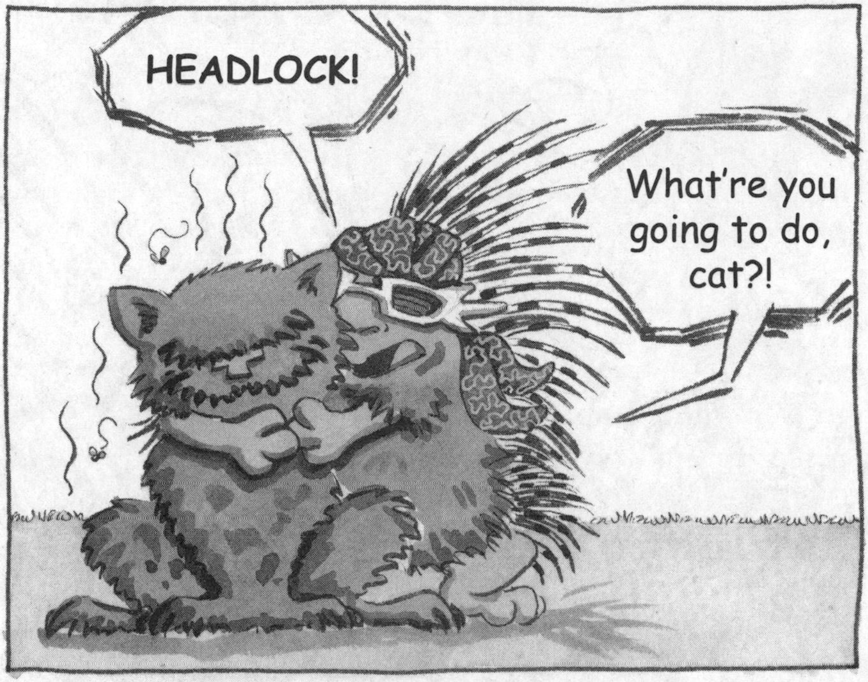
HEADLOCK!
What're you going to do, cat?!

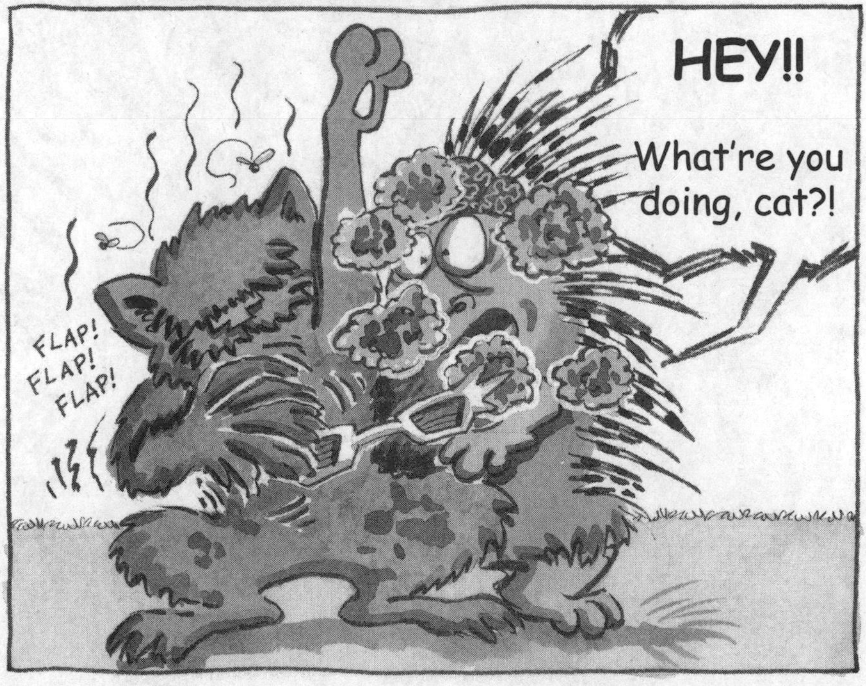
HEY!!
What're you doing, cat?!
FLAP! FLAP! FLAP!

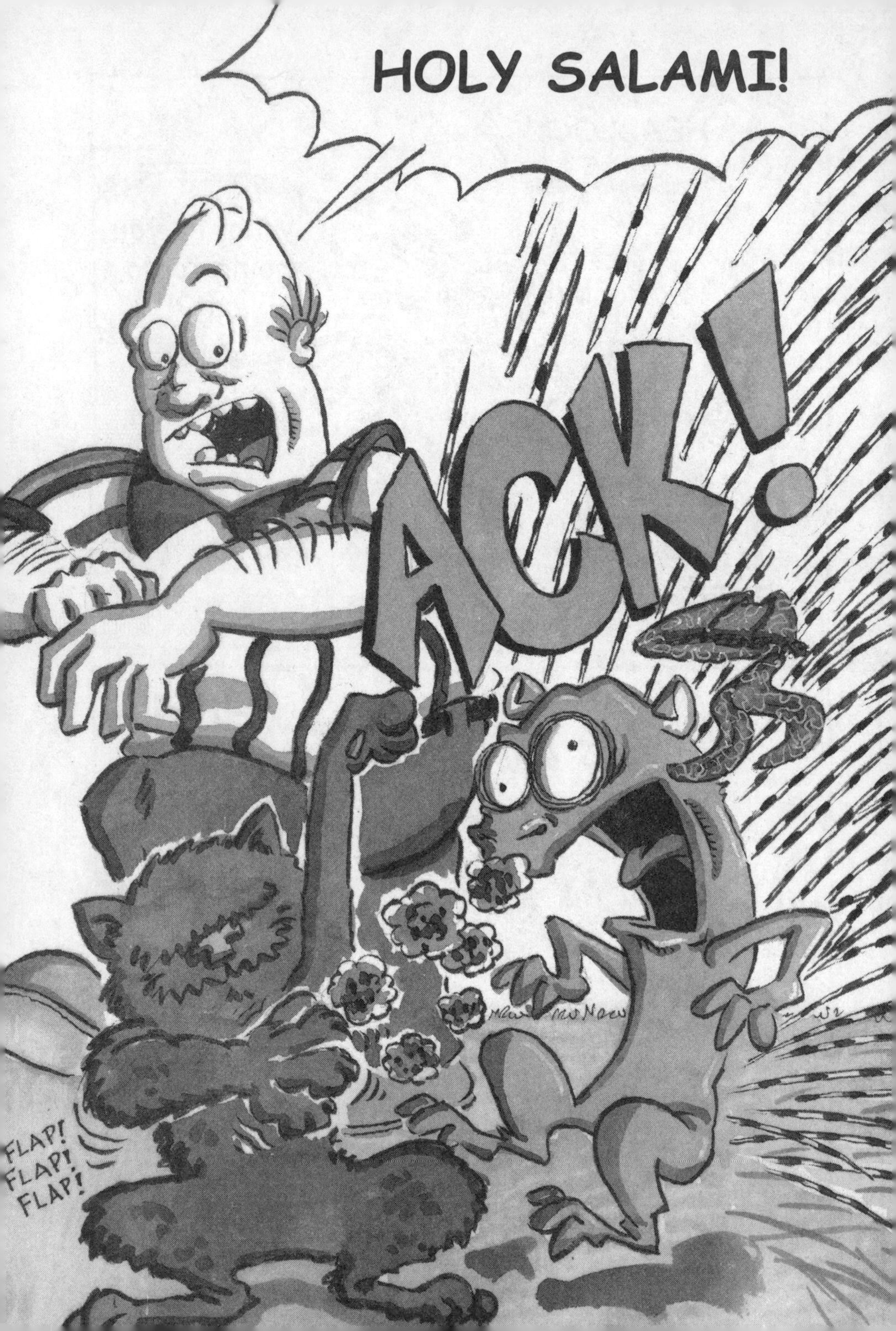
HOLY SALAMI!
ACK!
FLAP!
FLAP!
FLAP!

MEANWHILE . . . KITTY

Kitty, sometimes the games we play
are also a great way to exercise.
Like jump rope!

Try it, Kitty!

65

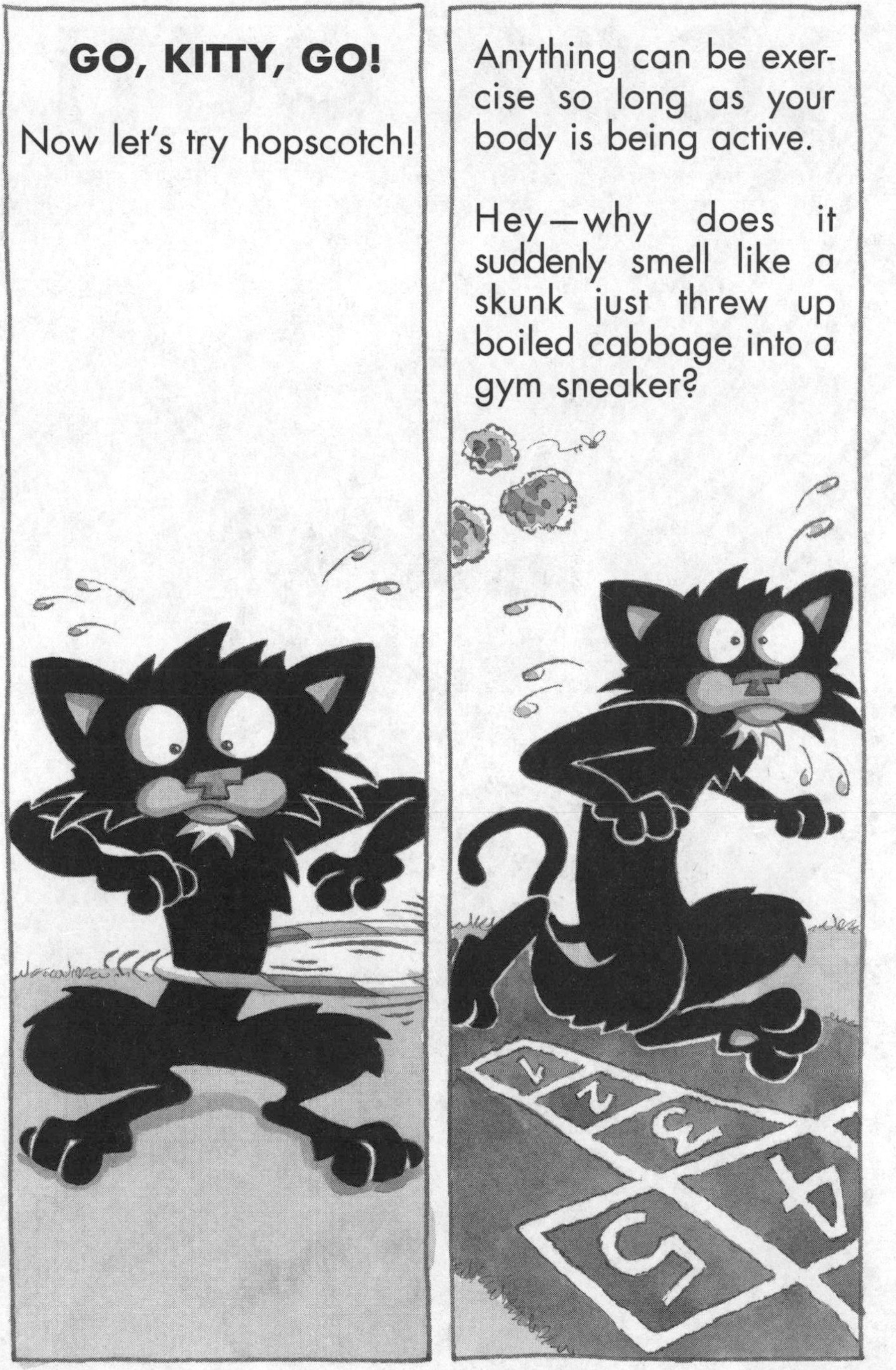
GO, KITTY, GO!
Now let's try hopscotch!
Anything can be exercise so long as your body is being active.
Hey—why does it suddenly smell like a skunk just threw up boiled cabbage into a gym sneaker?

LOOK OUT!

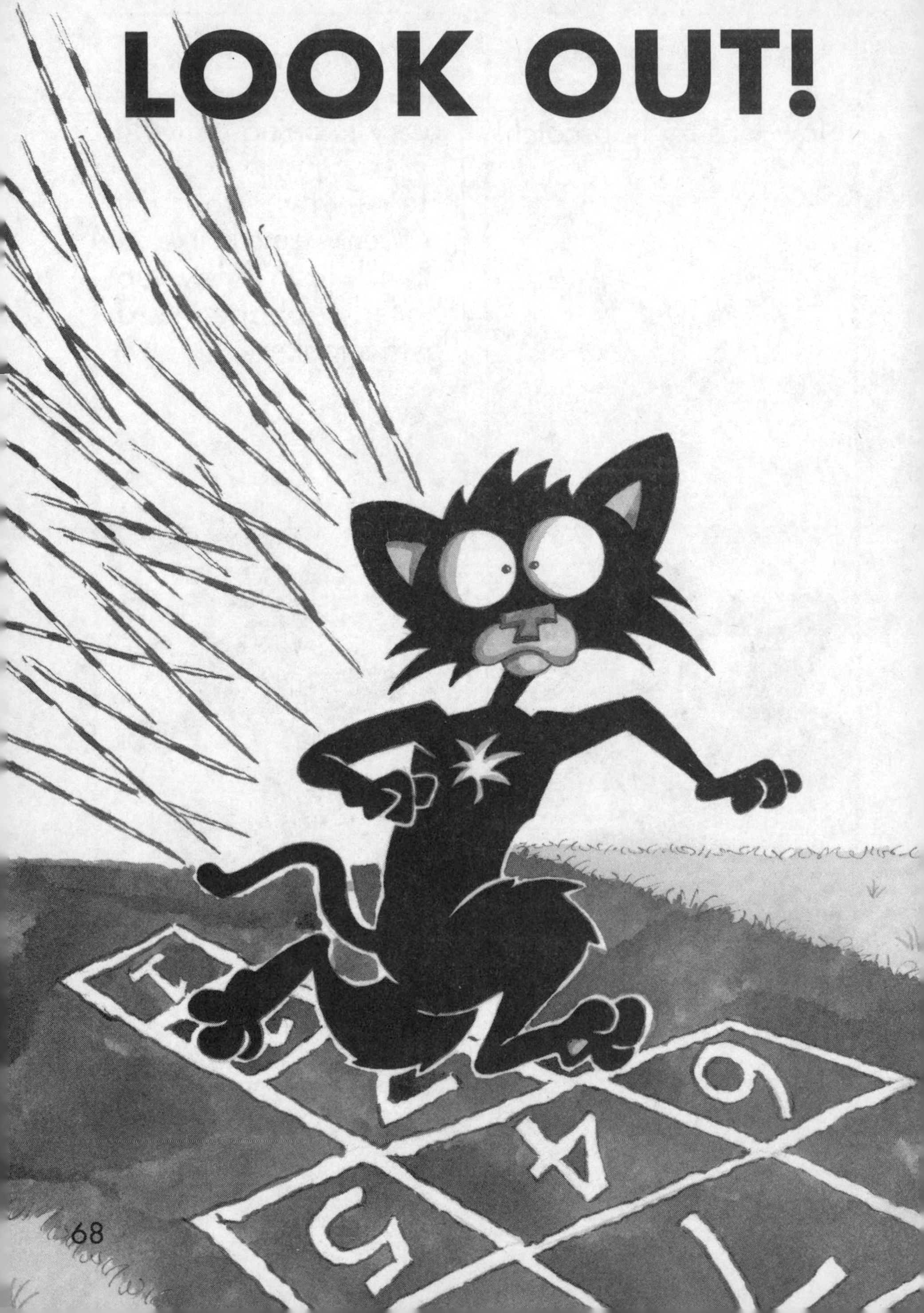

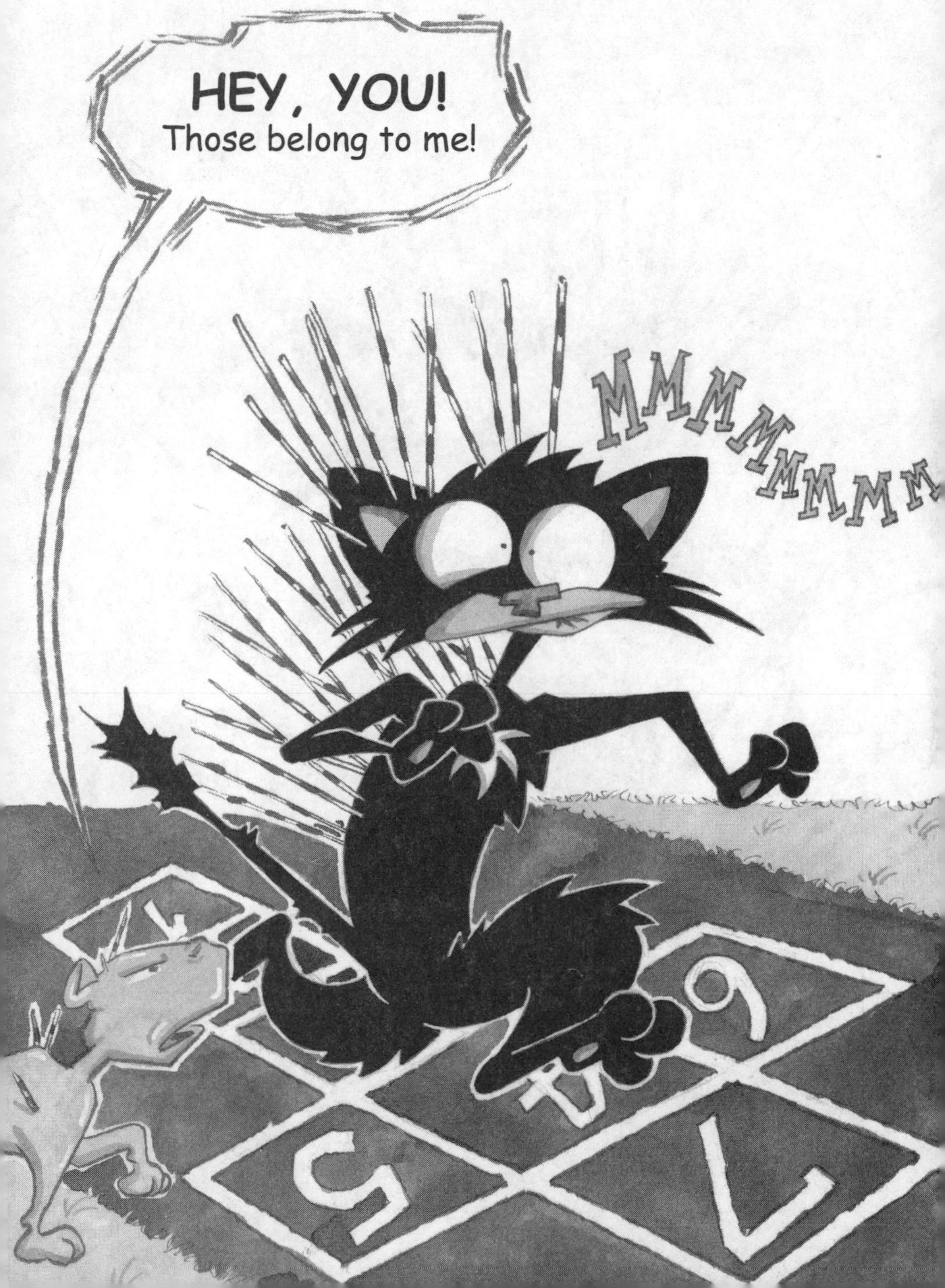
HEY, YOU!
Those belong to me!
MMMMMMMMMM

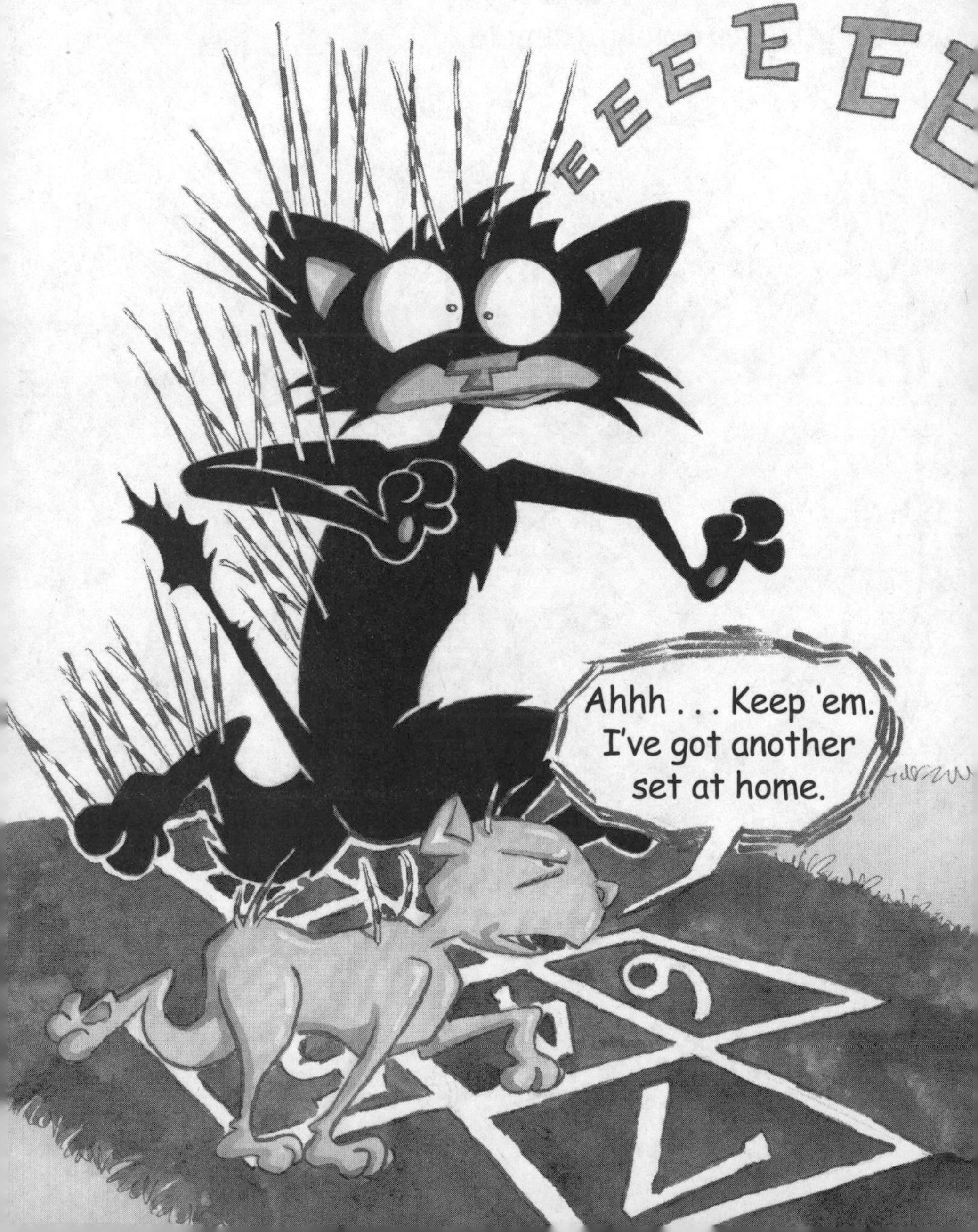
EEEEEE
Ahhh . . . Keep 'em. I've got another set at home.

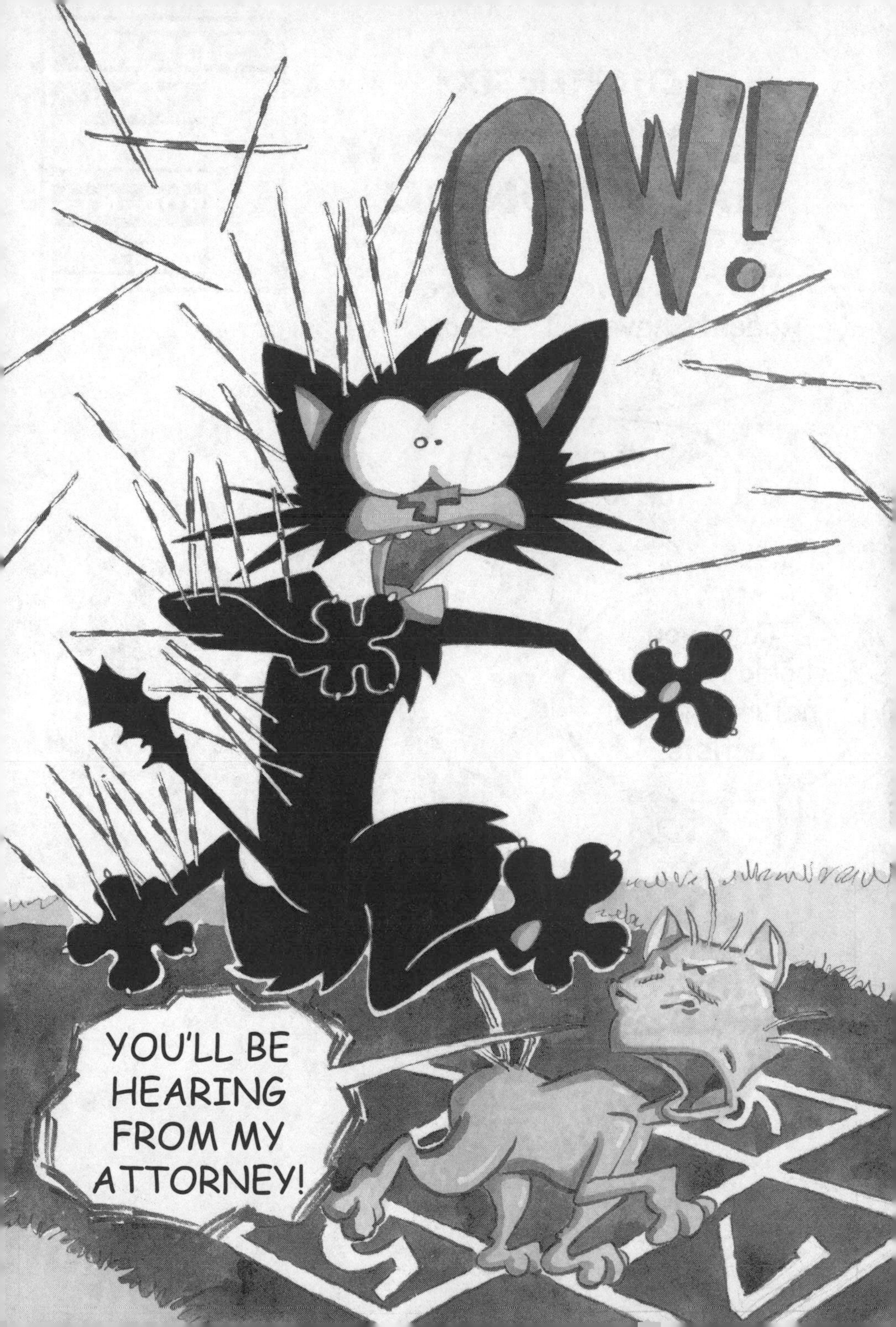
OW!
YOU'LL BE HEARING FROM MY ATTORNEY!

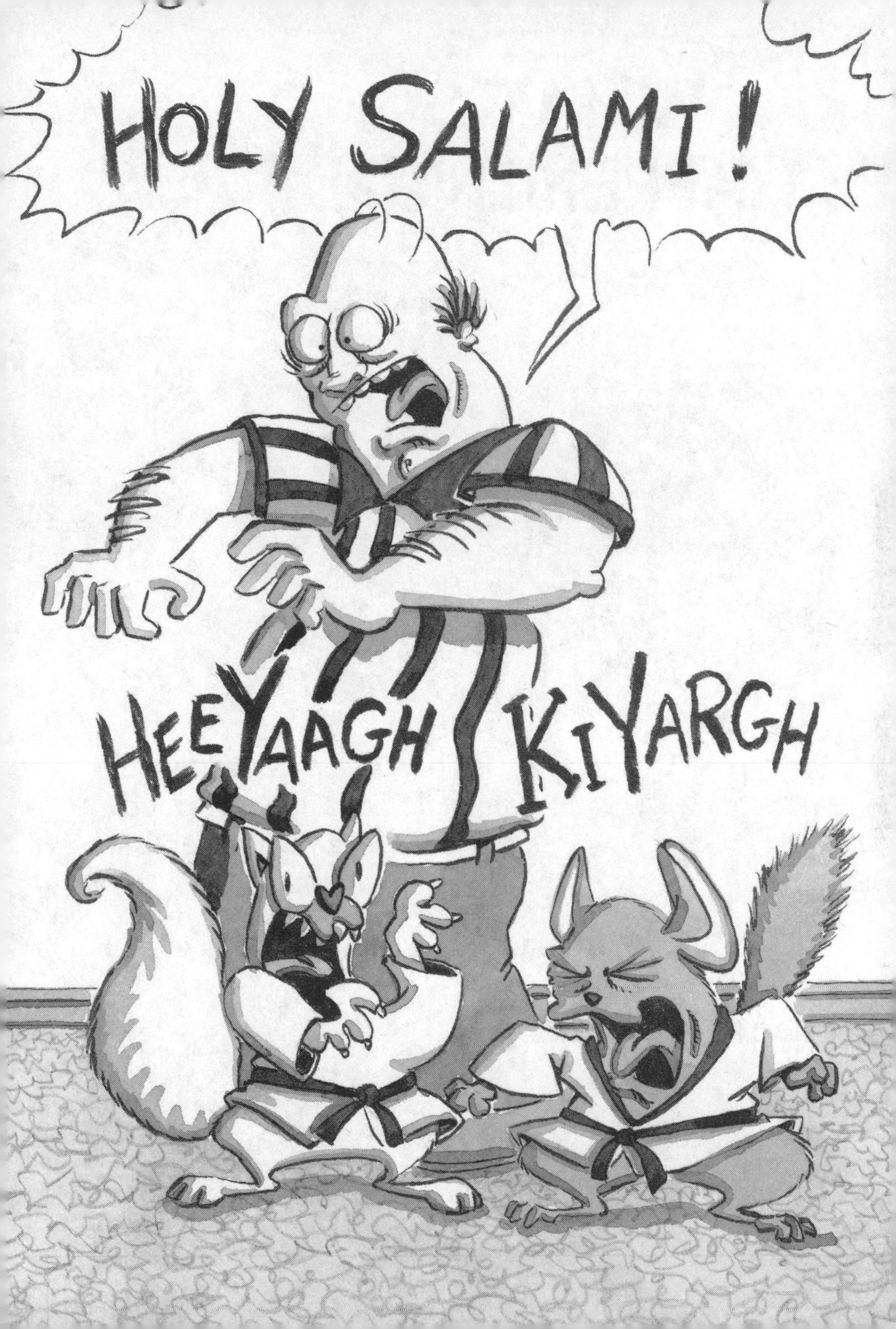
HOLY SALAMI!
HEEYAAGH
KIYARGH

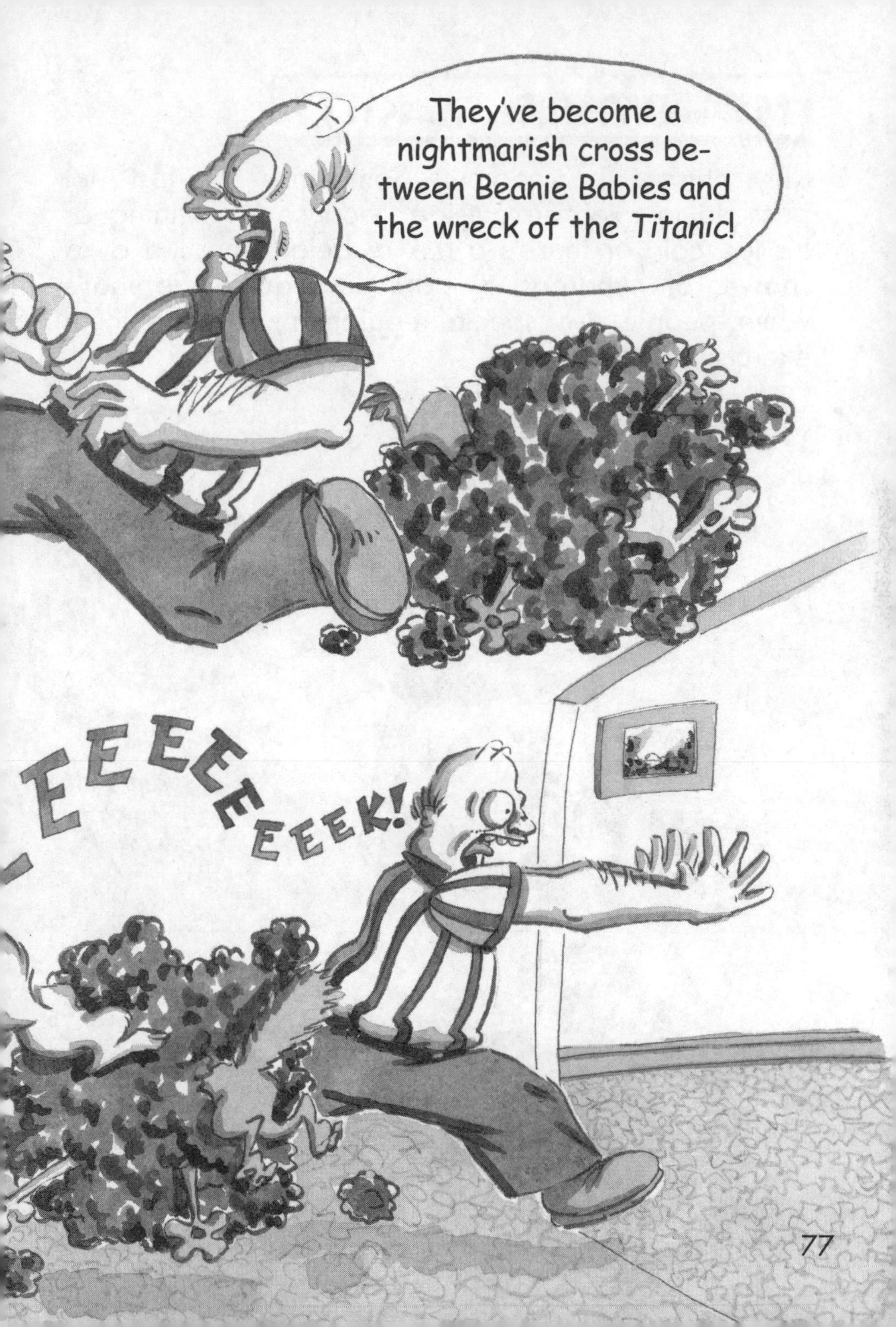
They've become a nightmarish cross between Beanie Babies and the wreck of the *Titanic*!
EEEEEEEEEEK!

MEANWHILE . . . KITTY

Kitty, this is a treadmill. Sometimes it's just not possible to exercise outside because it's raining or it's too cold or there's a risk of being impaled by a shower of hundreds of porcupine quills. So that's when people use special equipment to help them exercise inside.

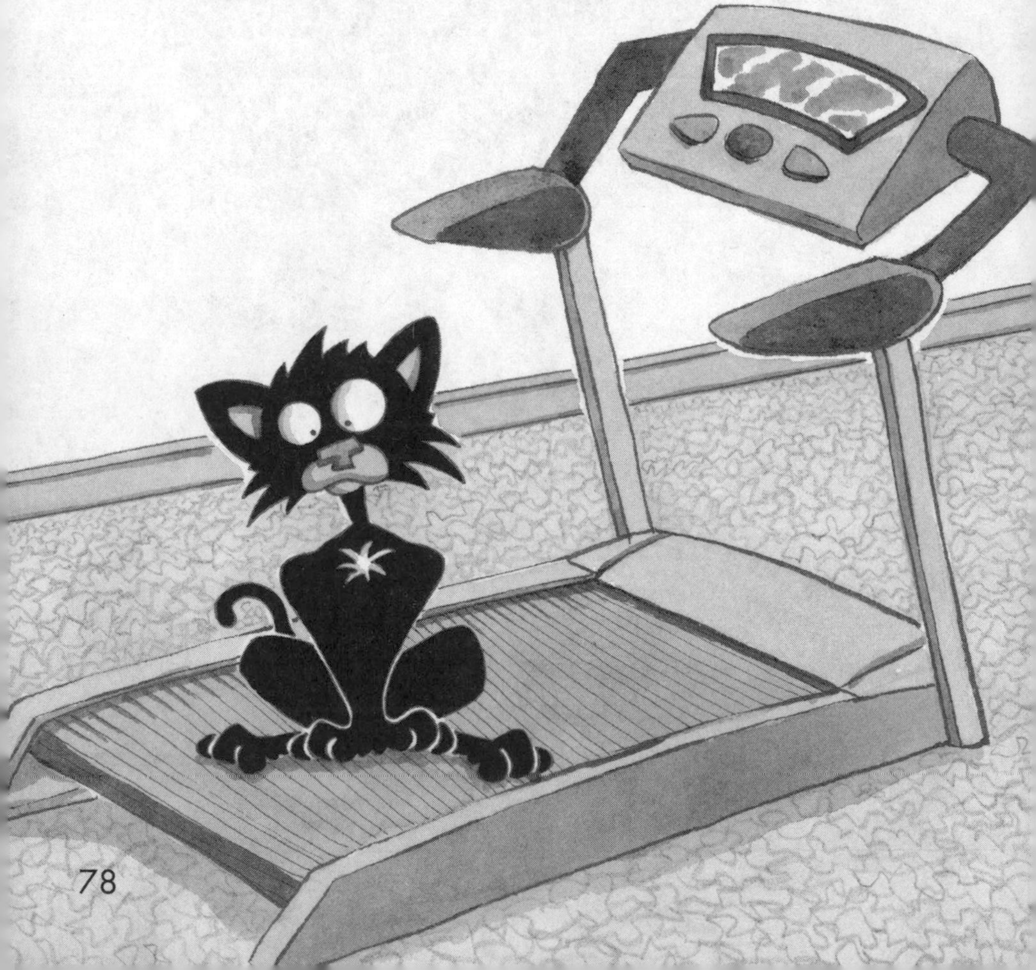

The track on the floor of this treadmill will move to make you feel like you're walking when you're really staying in one place.

There's similar exercise equipment to make you feel like you're riding a bike or climbing stairs or even rowing a boat.

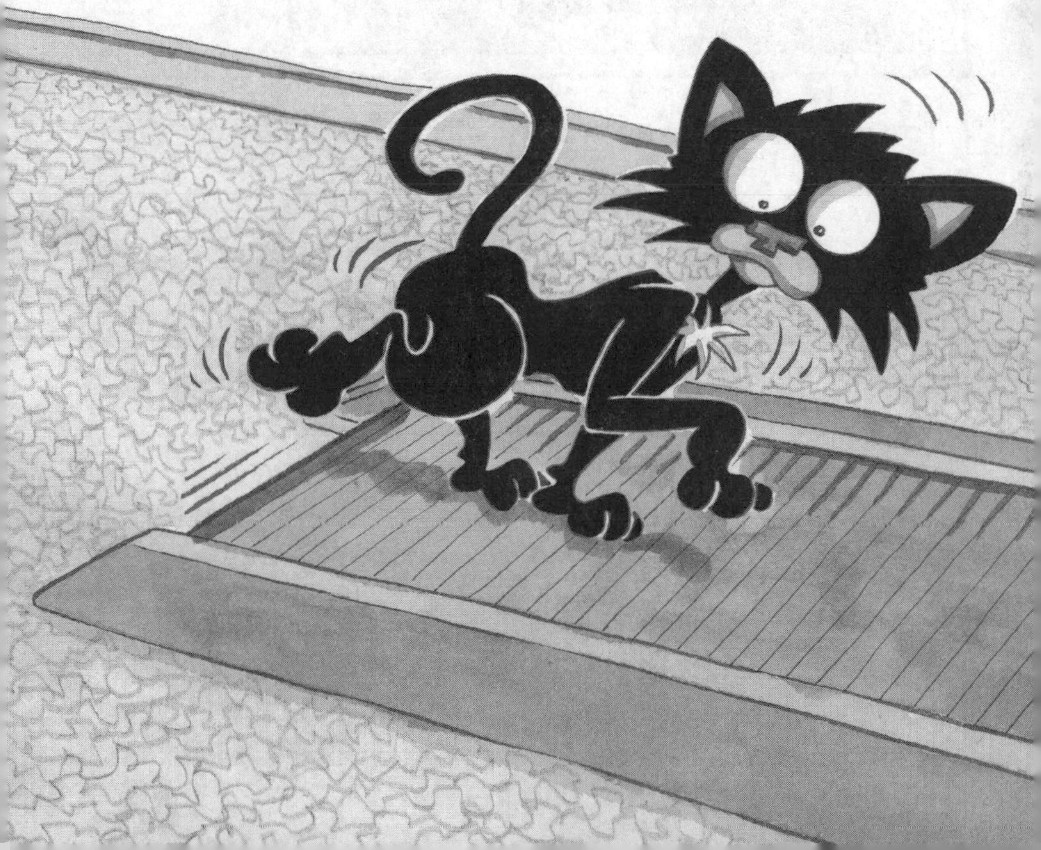

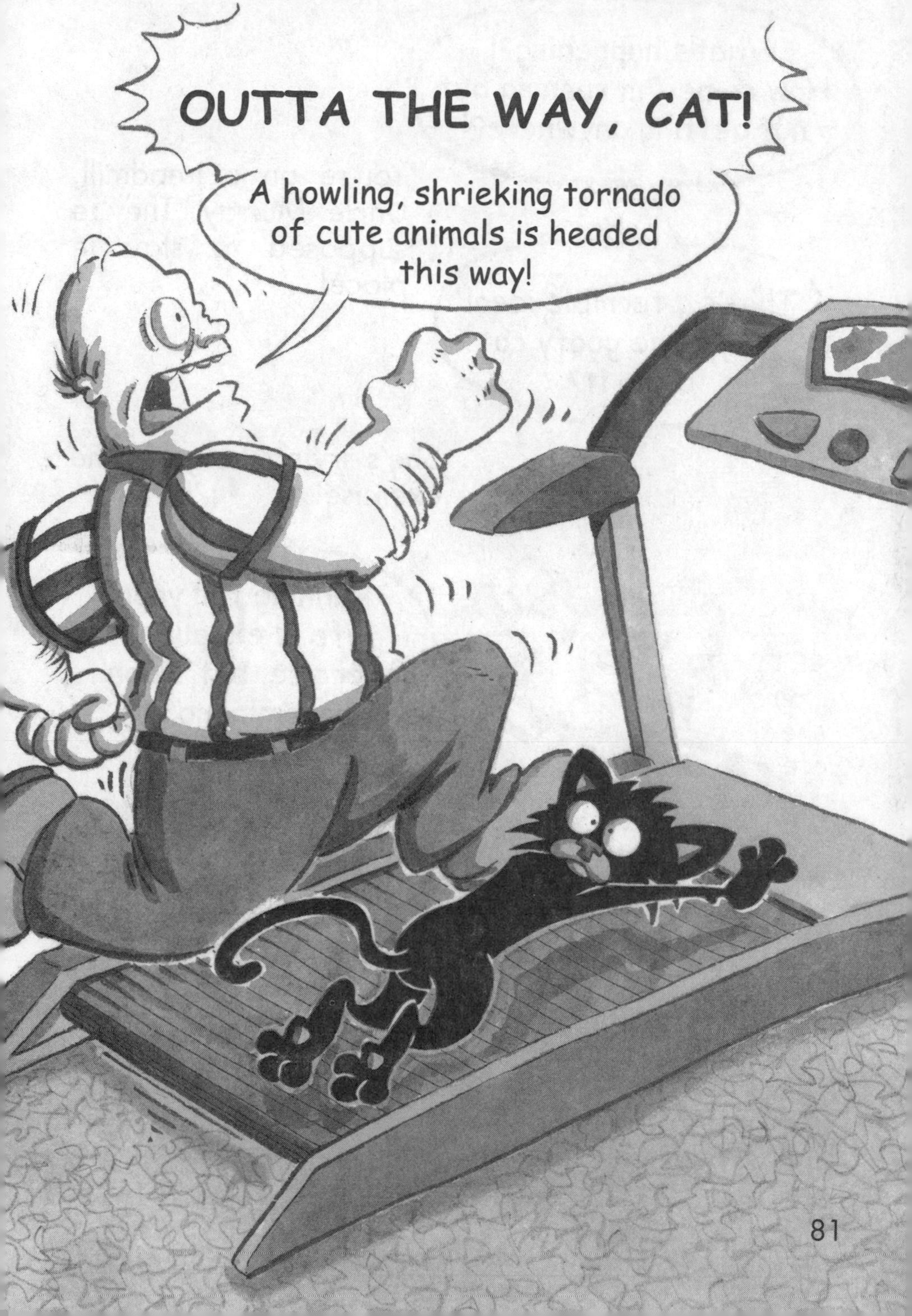
OUTTA THE WAY, CAT!
A howling, shrieking tornado of cute animals is headed this way!

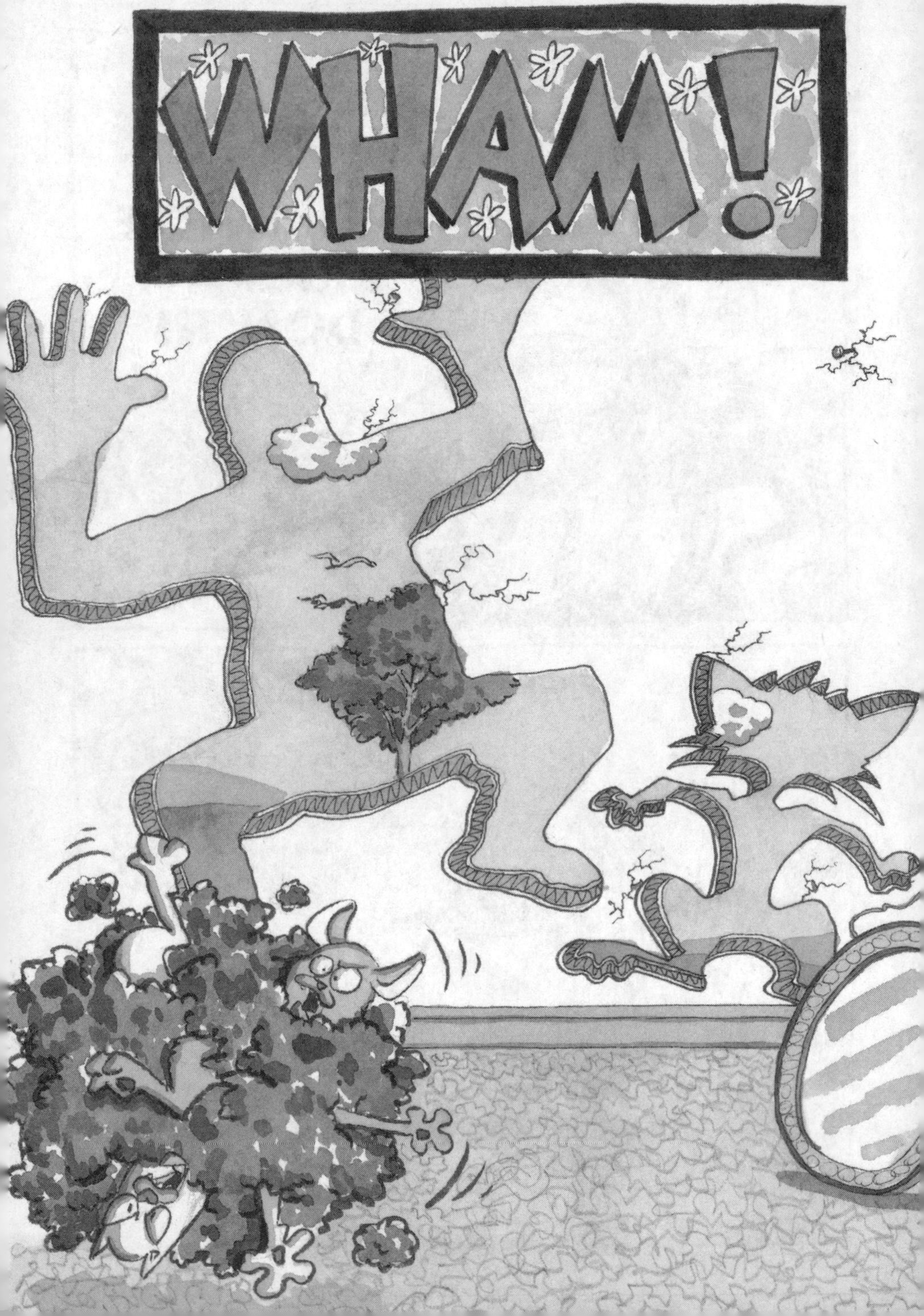
WHAM!

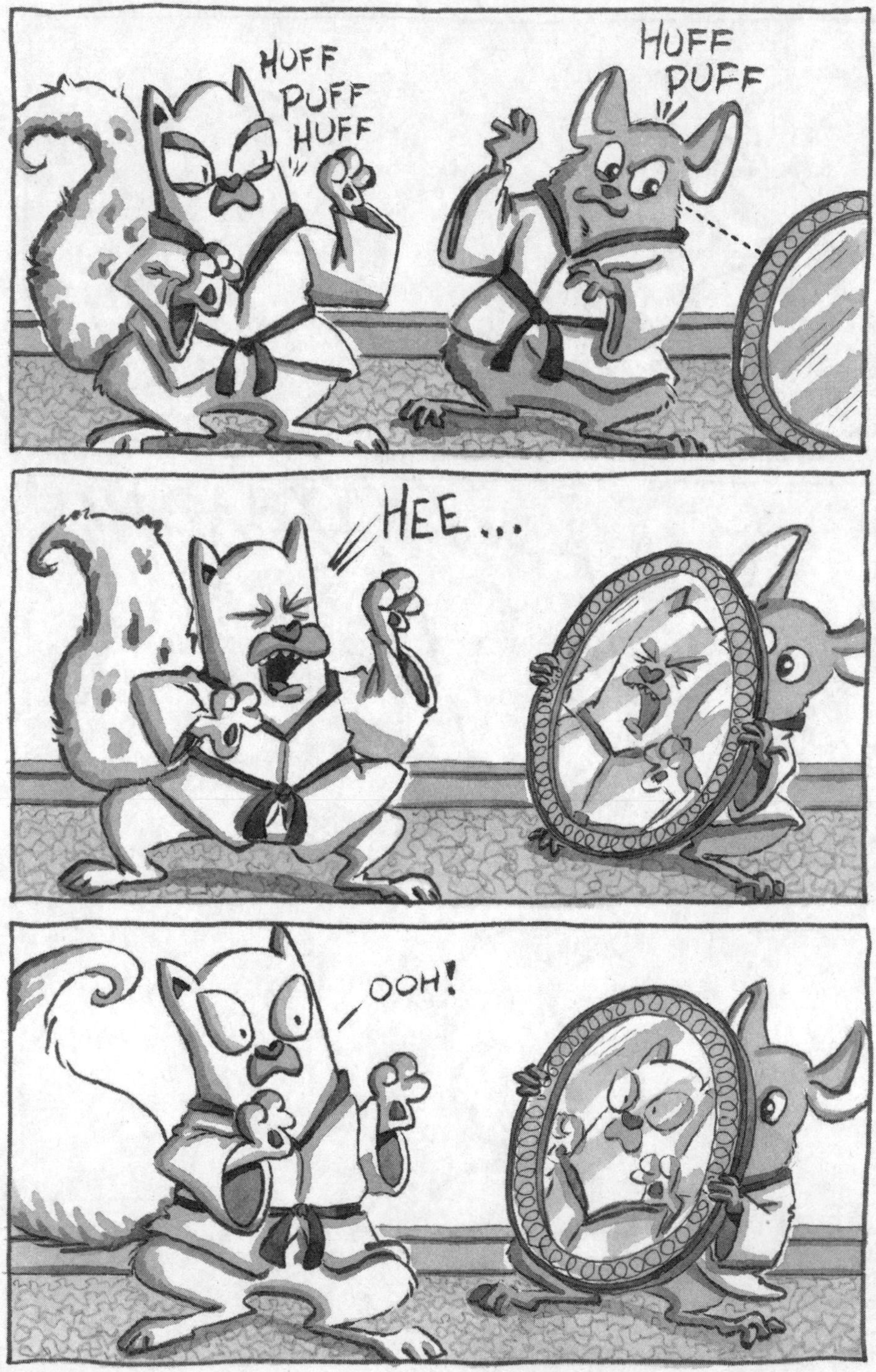
HUFF
PUFF
HUFF
HUFF
PUFF
HEE...
OOH!

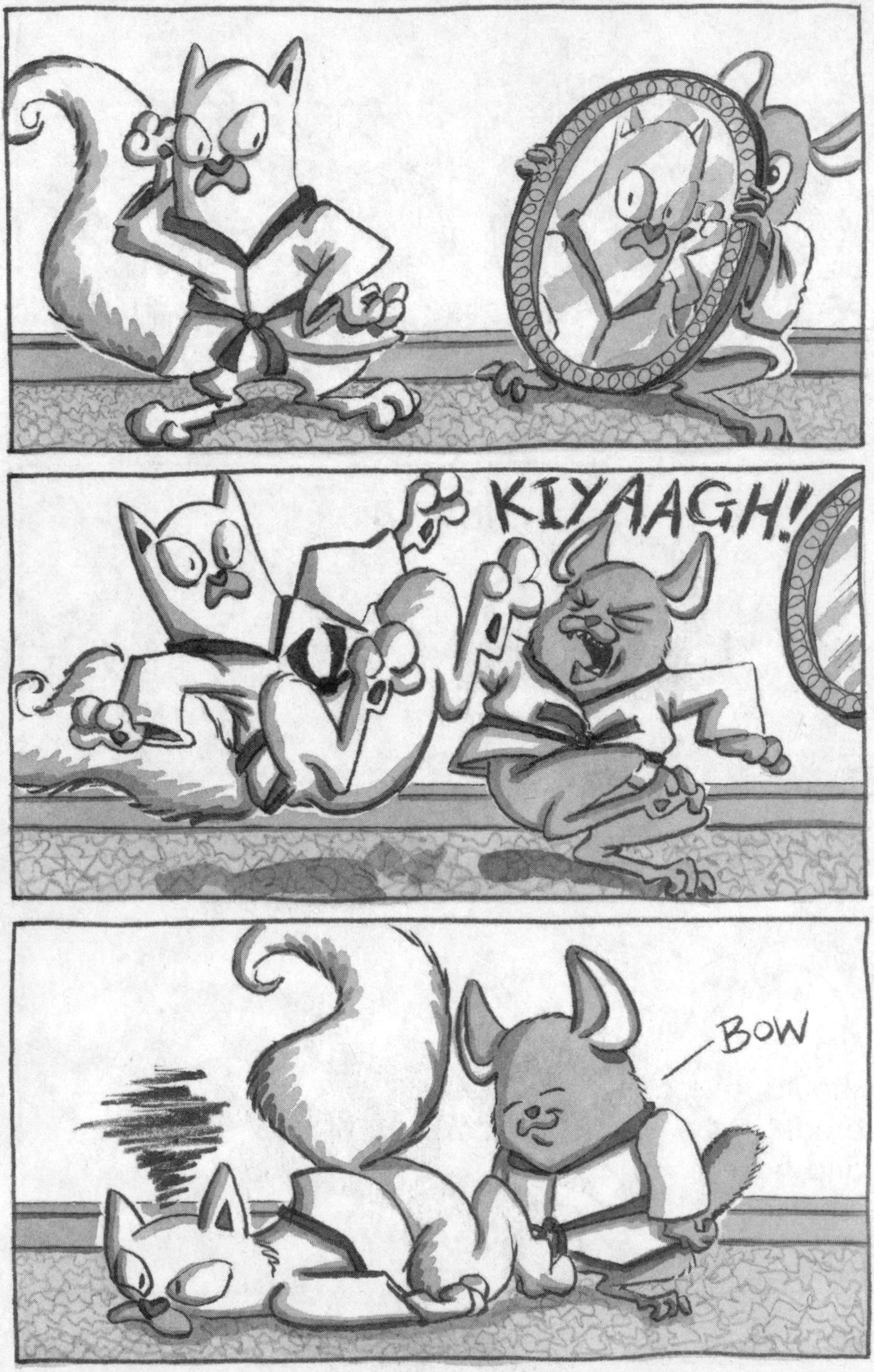
KIYAAGH!
BOW

CHAPTER SEVEN

THE FOURTH EVENT: GYMNASTICS

Next up—gymnastics! That should be nice and peaceful, right? No fighting. No biting. No collisions with the wall.

There's a reason that graceful people are called "catlike" and not "mouselike."

Your trash talk is so lame, it needs crutches!

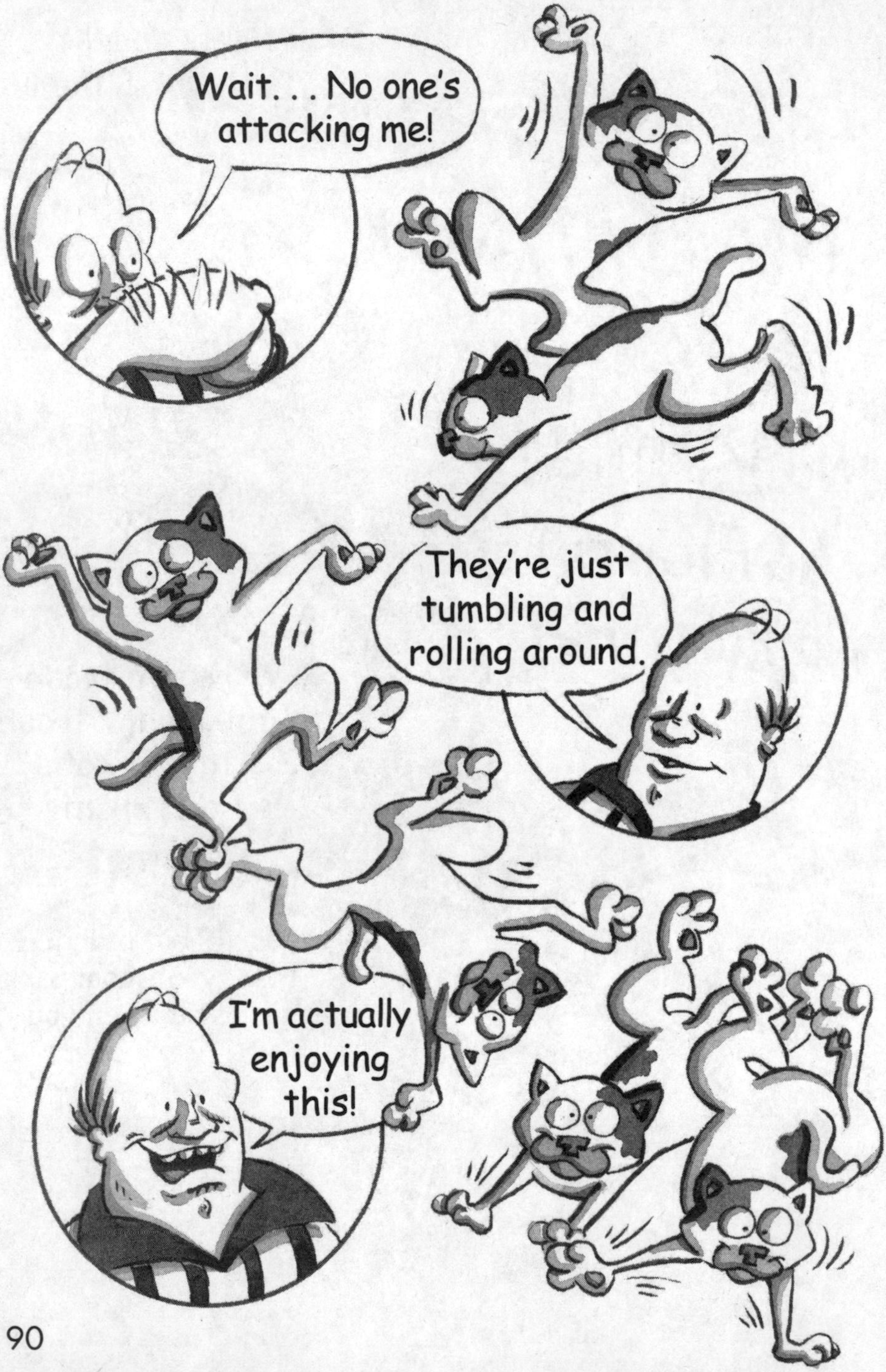
Wait. . . No one's attacking me!
They're just tumbling and rolling around.
I'm actually enjoying this!

91

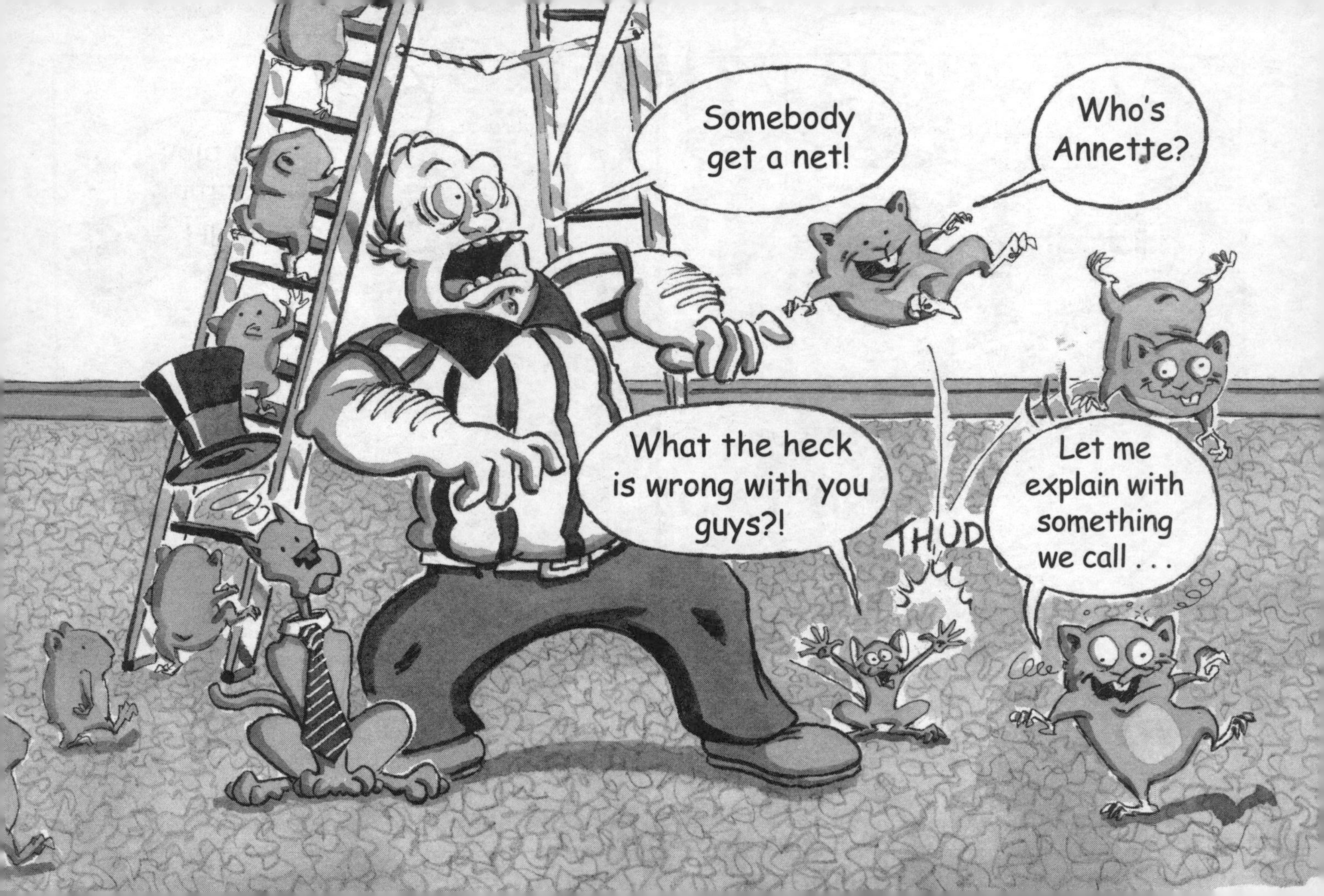
Somebody get a net!
Who's Annette?
What the heck is wrong with you guys?!
THUD
Let me explain with something we call . . .

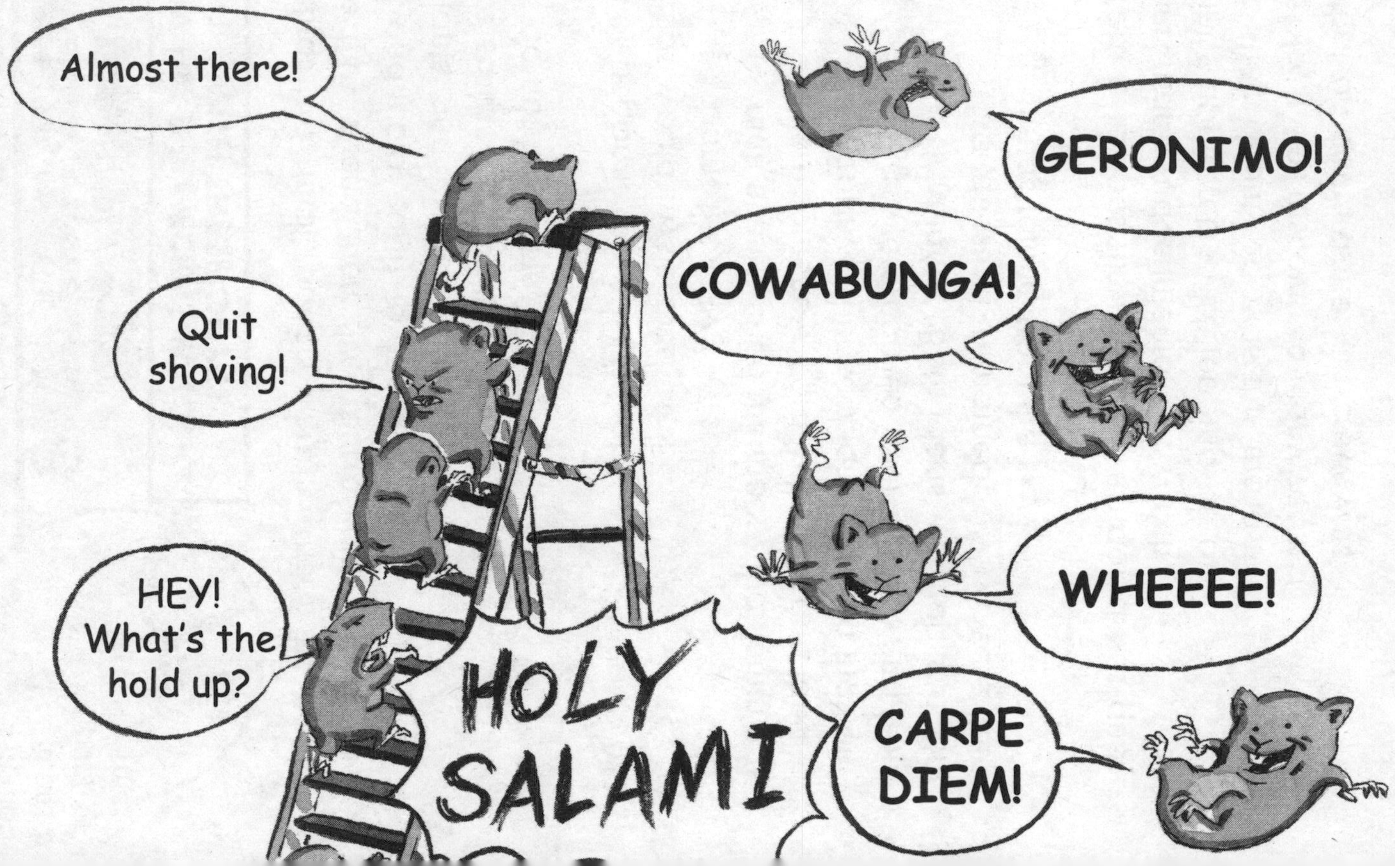
Almost there!
Quit shoving!
HEY! What's the hold up?
HOLY SALAMI
GERONIMO!
COWABUNGA!
WHEEEE!
CARPE DIEM!

THE LEMMING BROS'

UNCLE MURRAY'S FUN FACTS

WHAT THE HECK IS WRONG WITH THESE GUYS?

This time I'm glad I'm not a part of this!

Lemmings are small rodents who live near the Arctic where they spend their lives burrowing through the snow and cold earth to forage for plants and berries. Because they're so used to the cold, Lemmings do not hibernate.

A rumor began in the 1500s that lemmings would mysteriously fall from the sky. Wise men even formed the theory that lemmings were somehow born in the sky and landed on Earth. Other scholars believed that lemmings were carried over by the wind from distant lands. Both ideas were absurd. But the question remained: Why were lemmings falling from the sky?

In 1958, a famous film studio investigated this question and made a documentary in which lemmings appeared to be leaping off a cliff to their doom. So was this the answer? No. It was discovered many years later that off camera the film crew was pushing the lemmings over the edge. The film was a lie, but it created a rumor that lemmings regularly leap off cliffs on purpose. The TRUTH is that lemmings reproduce very quickly and are sometimes clumsy.

A lemming population can grow to be three thousand times its size in just four years. This is not surprising considering that a female lemming can become pregnant at just two weeks old. During those times where there are too many lemmings for even the lemmings to be comfortable, they disperse. They travel in every direction to find more room, more food, and new homes.

Sometimes their travels will take them to lakes and rivers. But they don't stop. They push ahead and swim, even if some of them don't make it across.

And sometimes their travels will take them to steep slopes where, not being terribly agile, they tumble and roll and sometimes accidentally fall off a cliff, possibly landing in front of a wise man from the 1500s who is confused by what he's just seen.

Keep the Fun Facts!
I just want a helmet!

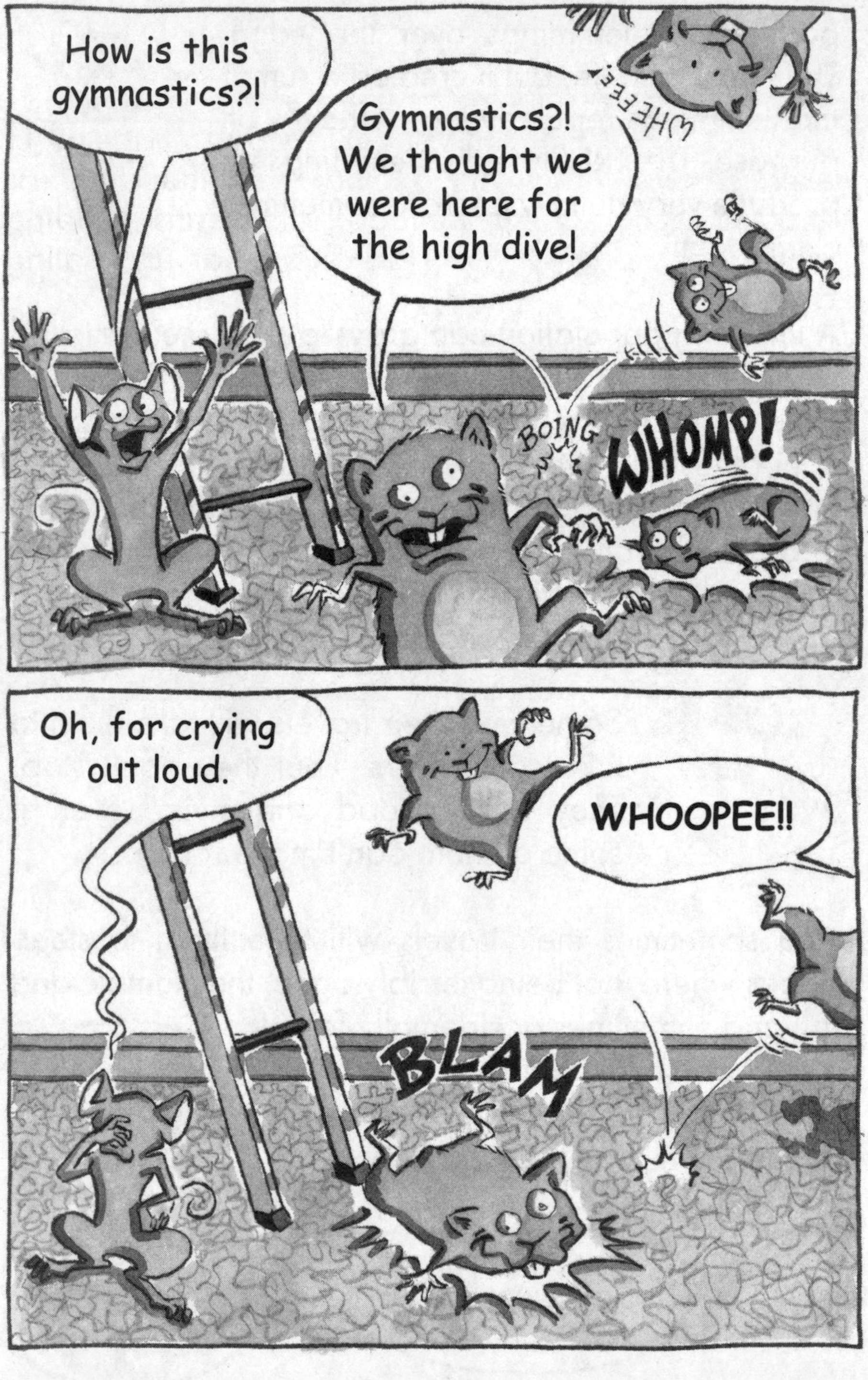
How is this gymnastics?!
Gymnastics?! We thought we were here for the high dive!
WHEEEE!
BOING
WHOMP!
Oh, for crying out loud.
WHOOPEE!!
BLAM

MEANWHILE . . . KITTY

One way to keep your body in good shape is to exercise every day. But another way that's just as important is to eat healthy food. This means avoiding foods that are heavy with fats and sugar and eating a balanced diet of meats, grains, fruits and . . .

VEGETABLES.

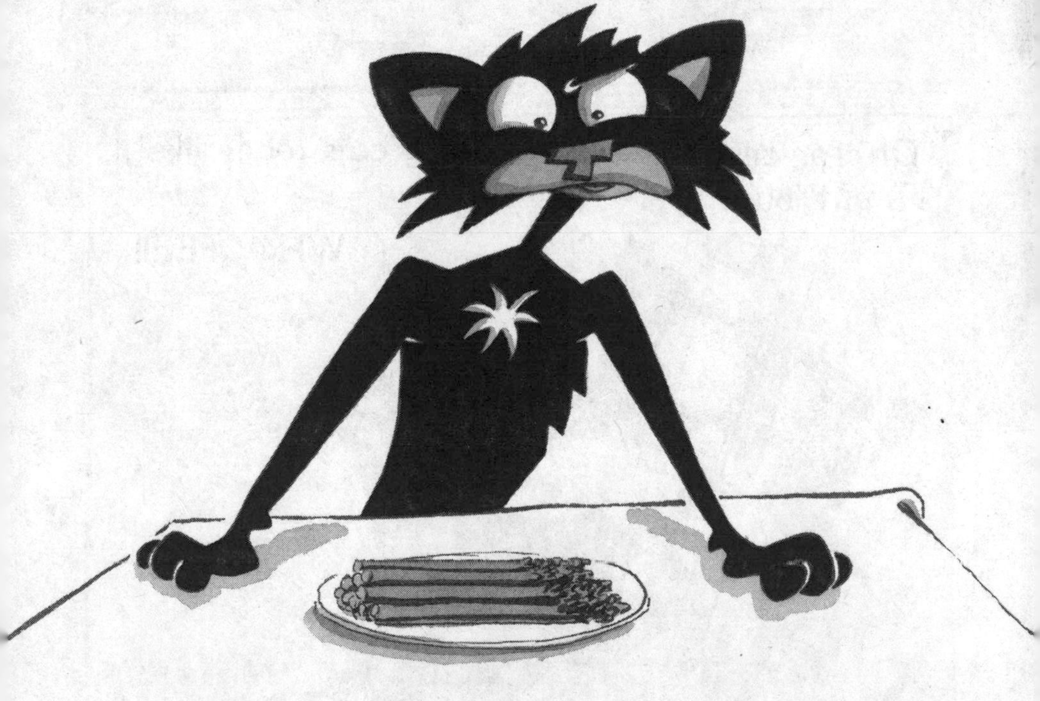

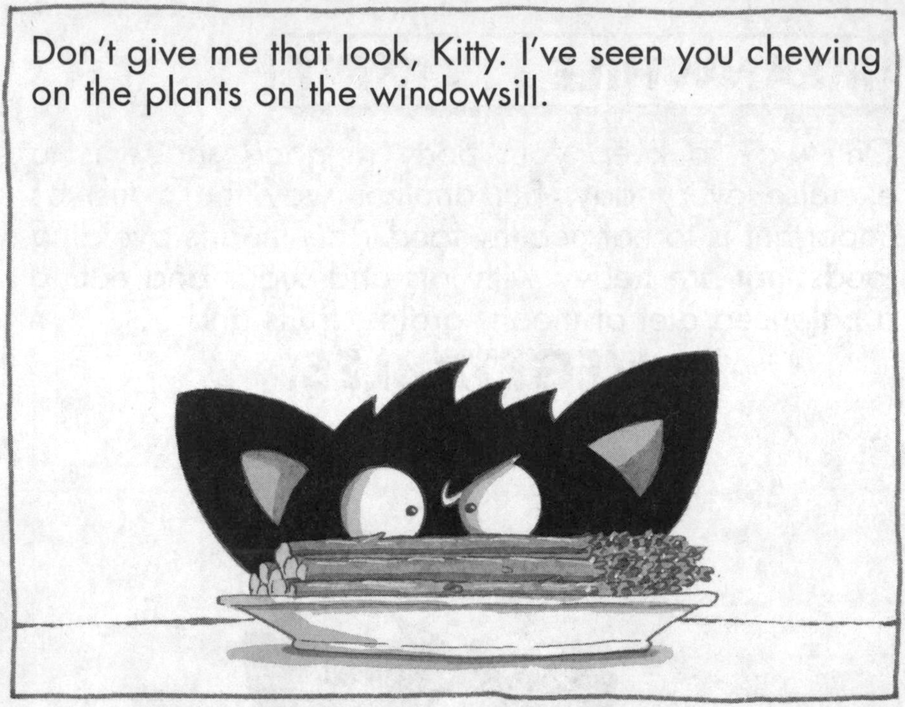
Don't give me that look, Kitty. I've seen you chewing on the plants on the windowsill.

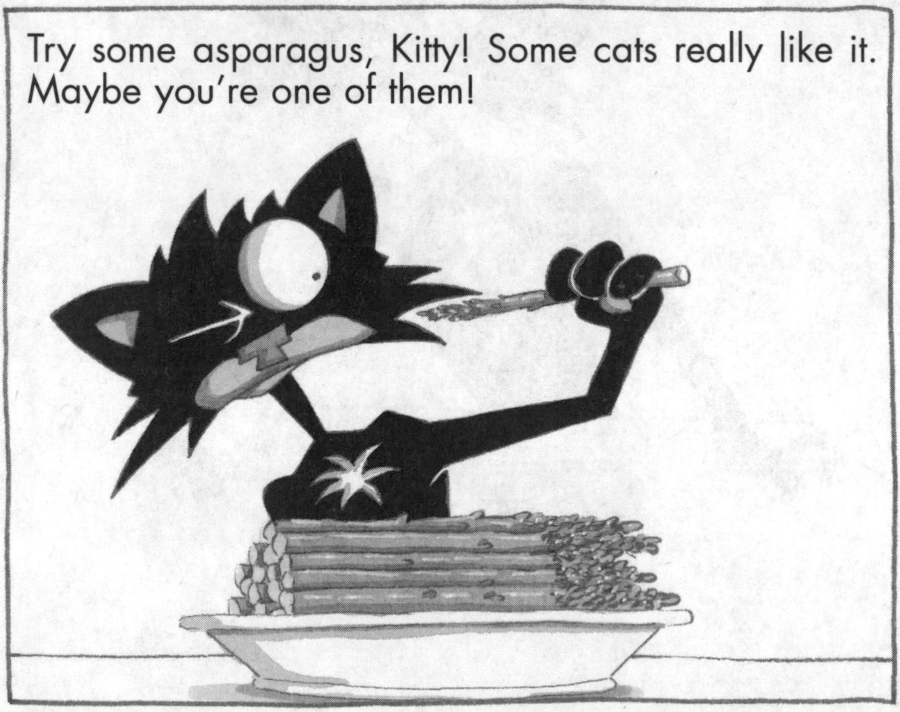
Try some asparagus, Kitty! Some cats really like it. Maybe you're one of them!

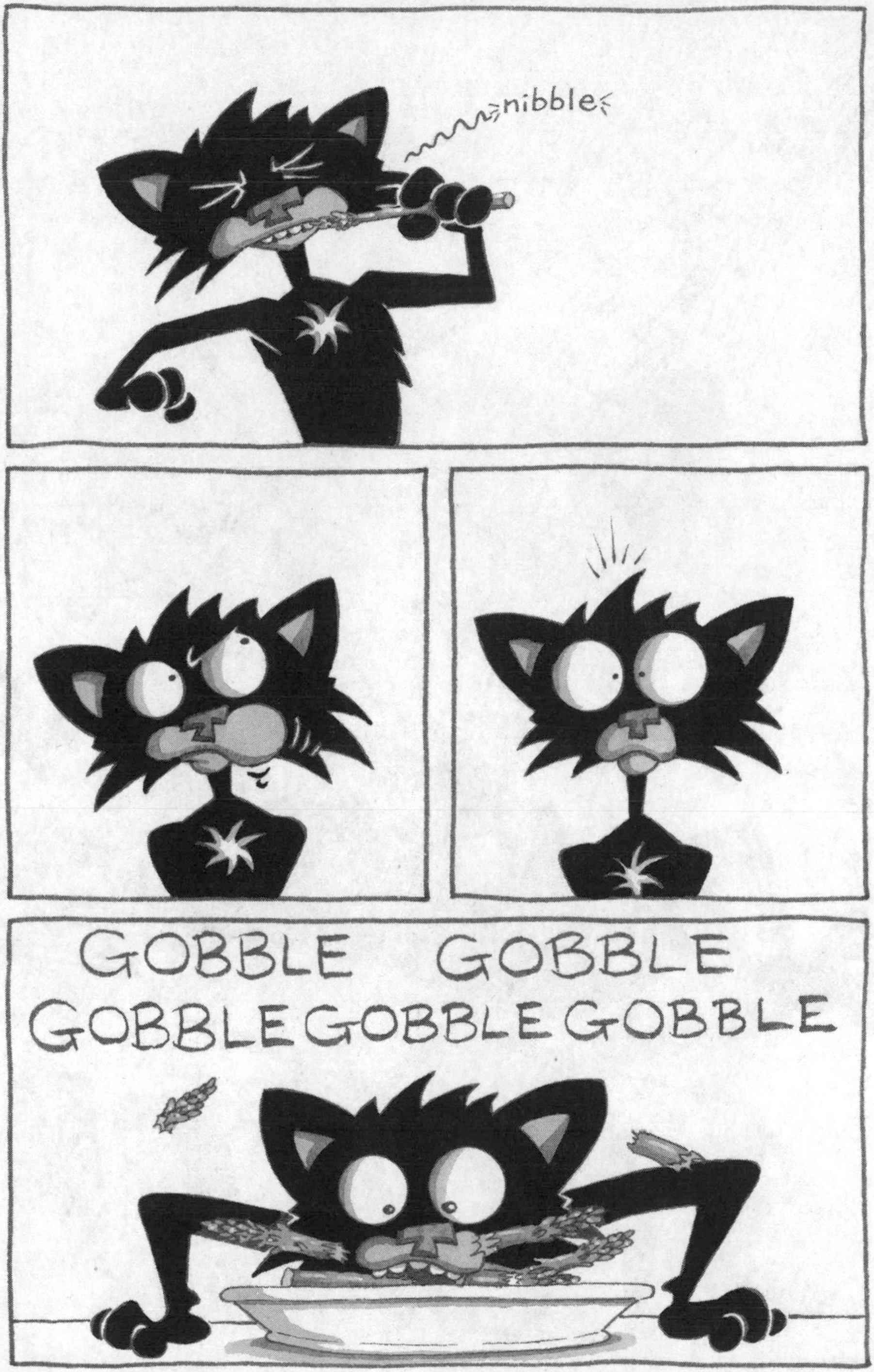
nibble
GOBBLE GOBBLE
GOBBLE GOBBLE GOBBLE

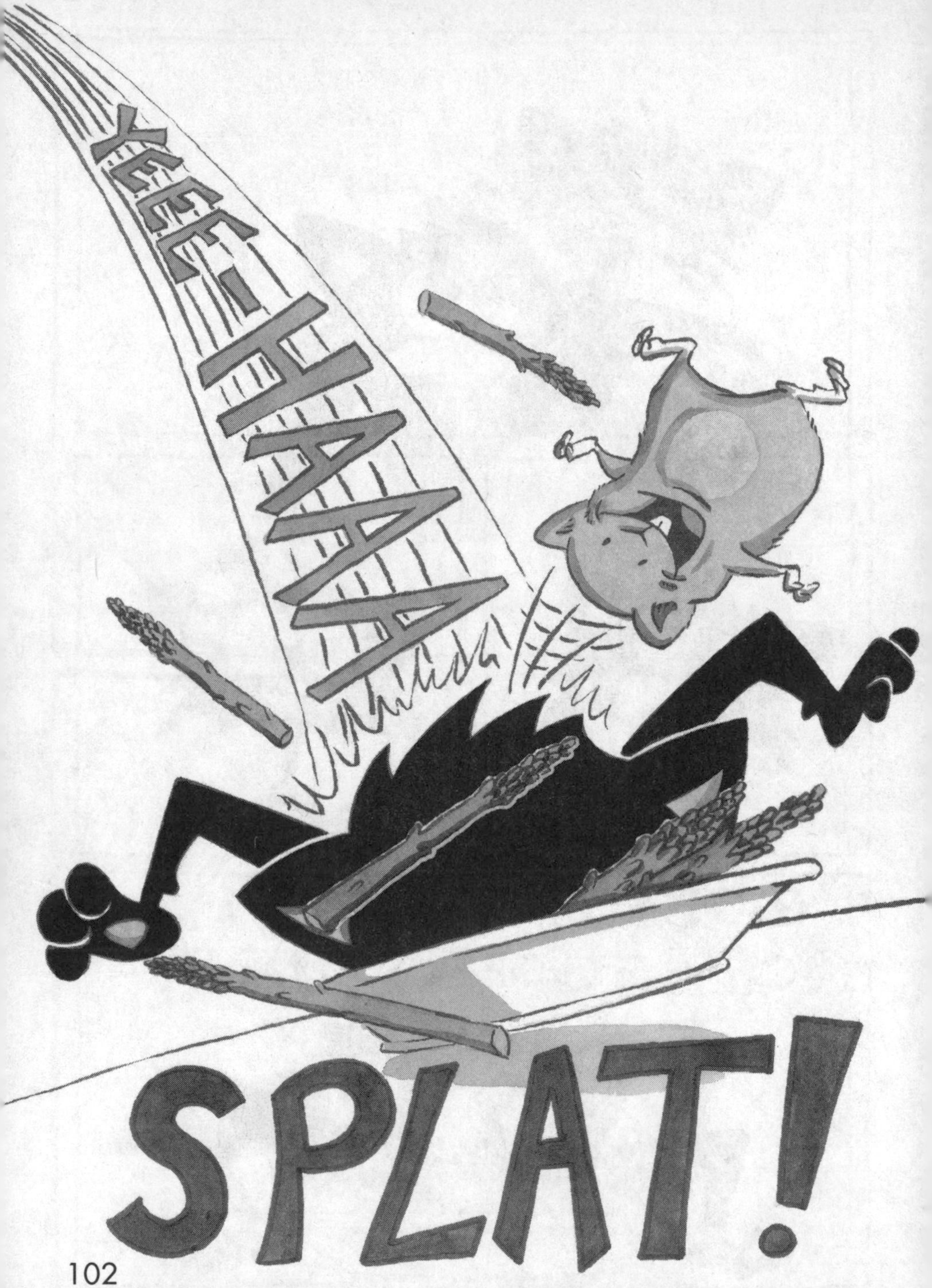
YEEE-HAAAA
SPLAT!

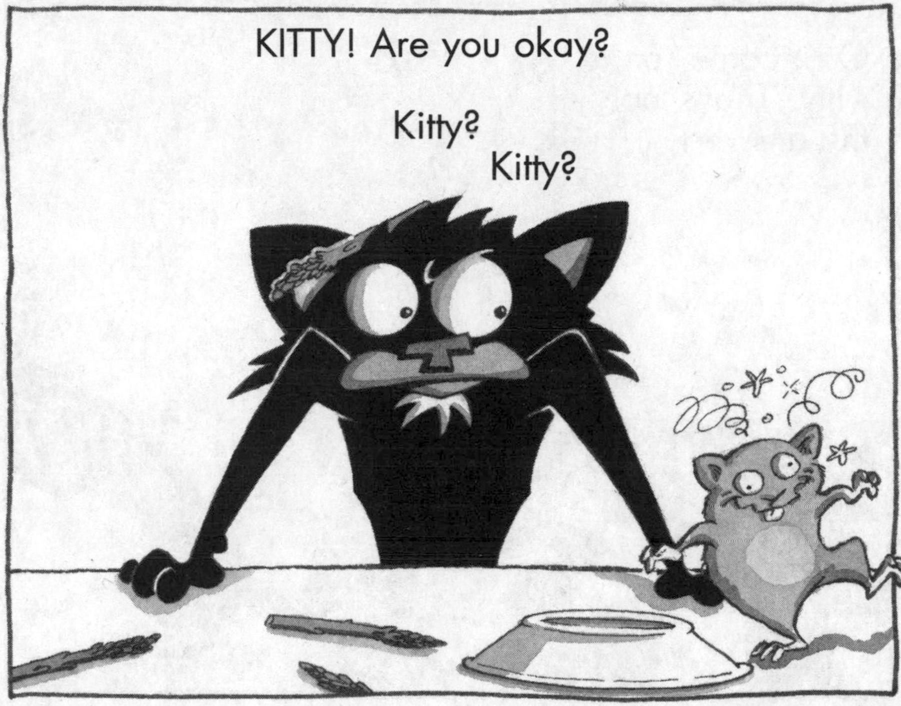
KITTY! Are you okay?
Kitty?
Kitty?

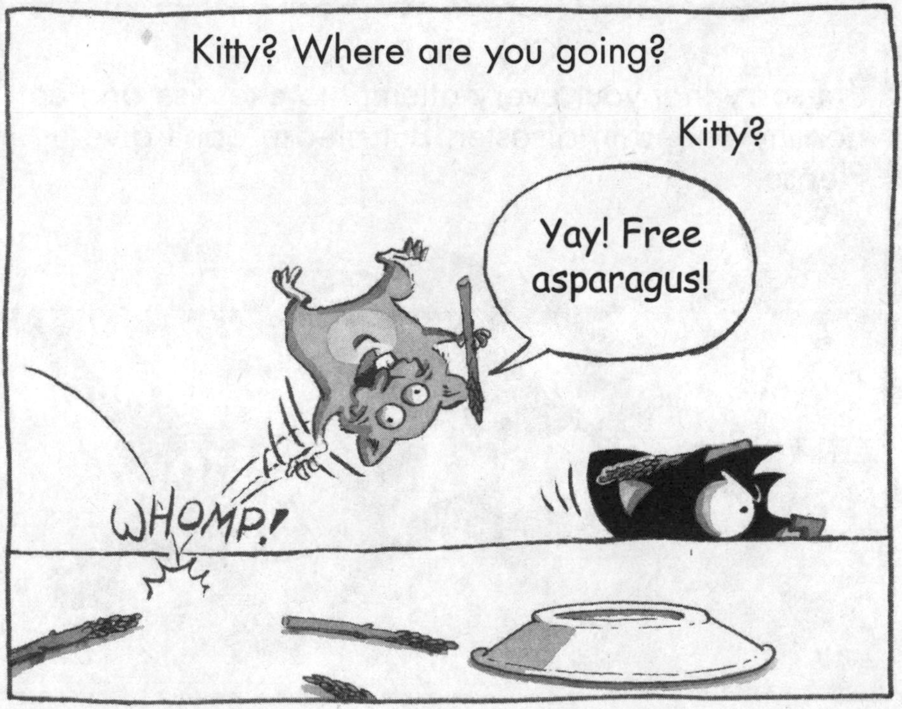
Kitty? Where are you going?
Kitty?
Yay! Free asparagus!
WHOMP!

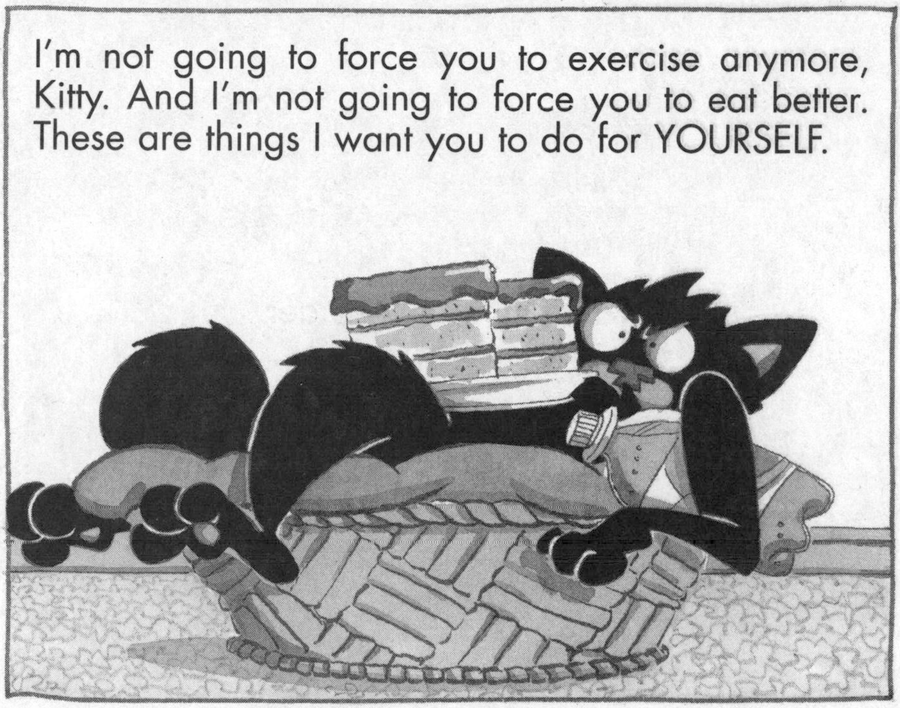
I'm not going to force you to exercise anymore, Kitty. And I'm not going to force you to eat better. These are things I want you to do for YOURSELF.

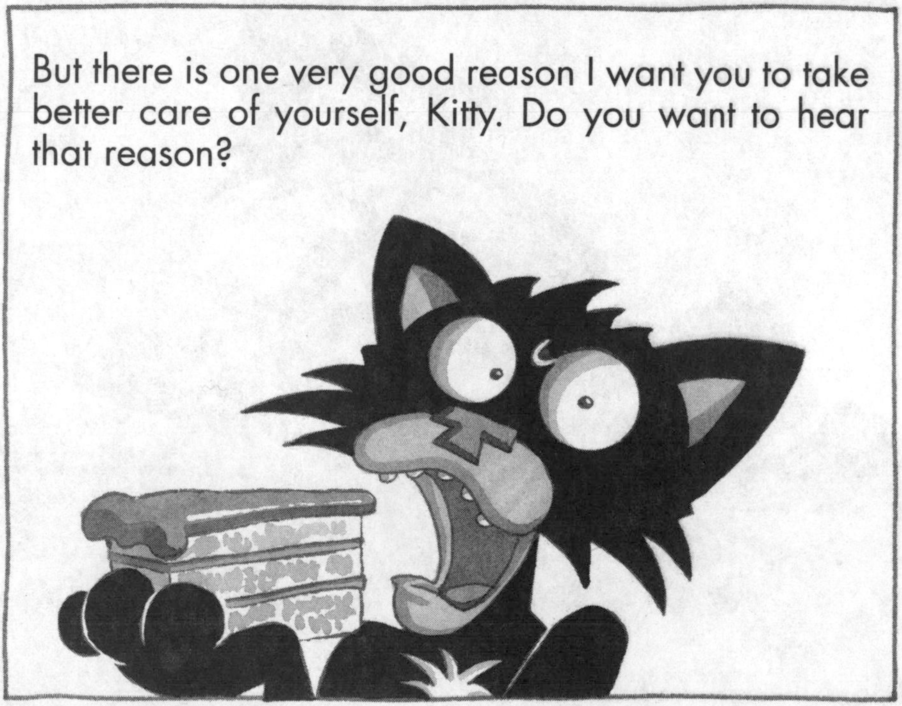
But there is one very good reason I want you to take better care of yourself, Kitty. Do you want to hear that reason?

I want you to live longer.

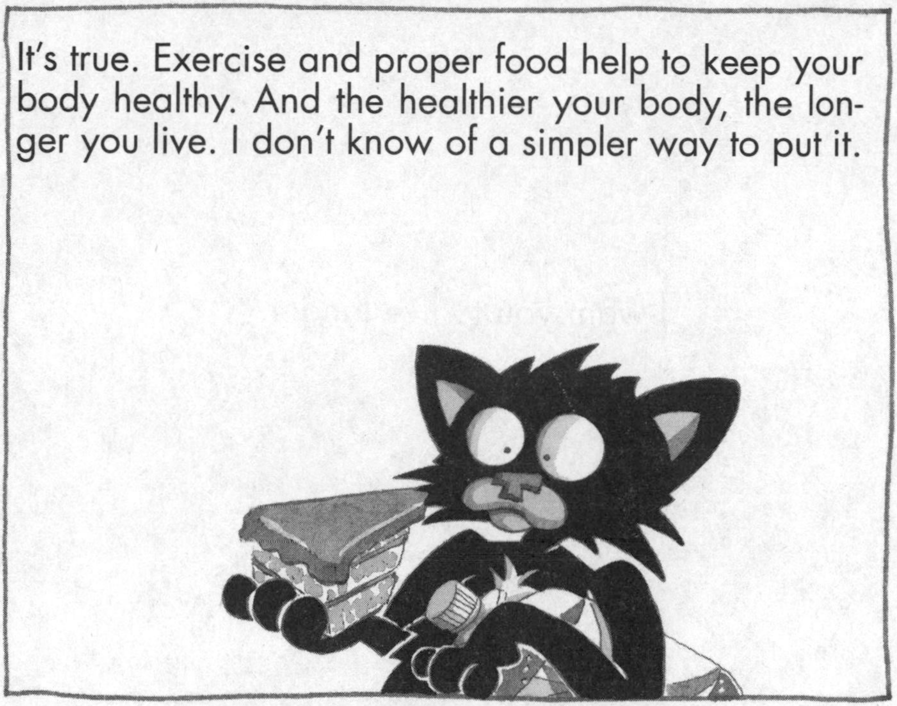
It's true. Exercise and proper food help to keep your body healthy. And the healthier your body, the longer you live. I don't know of a simpler way to put it.

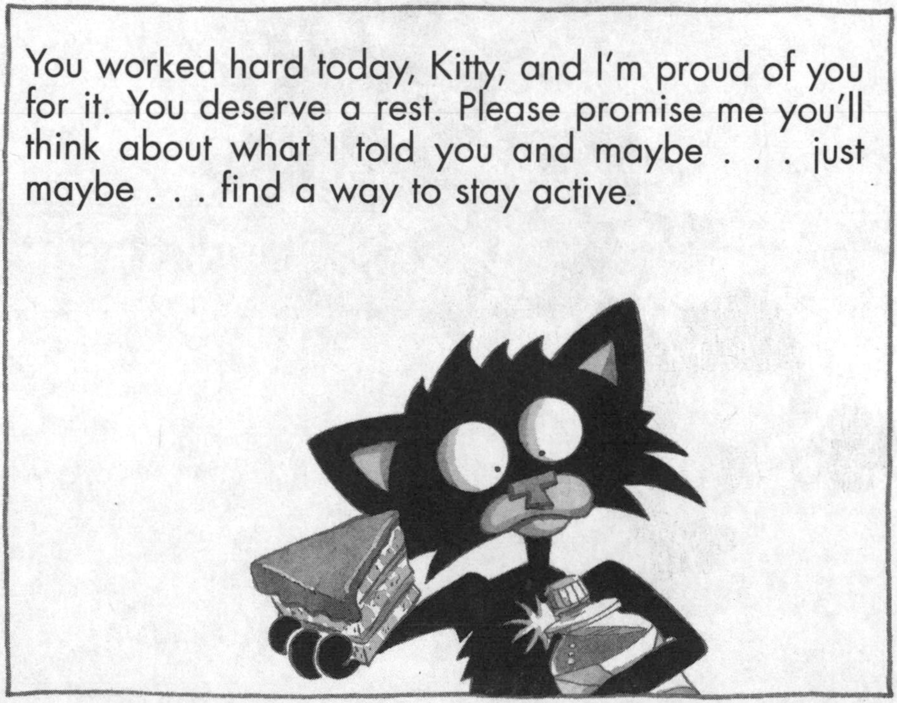
You worked hard today, Kitty, and I'm proud of you for it. You deserve a rest. Please promise me you'll think about what I told you and maybe . . . just maybe . . . find a way to stay active.

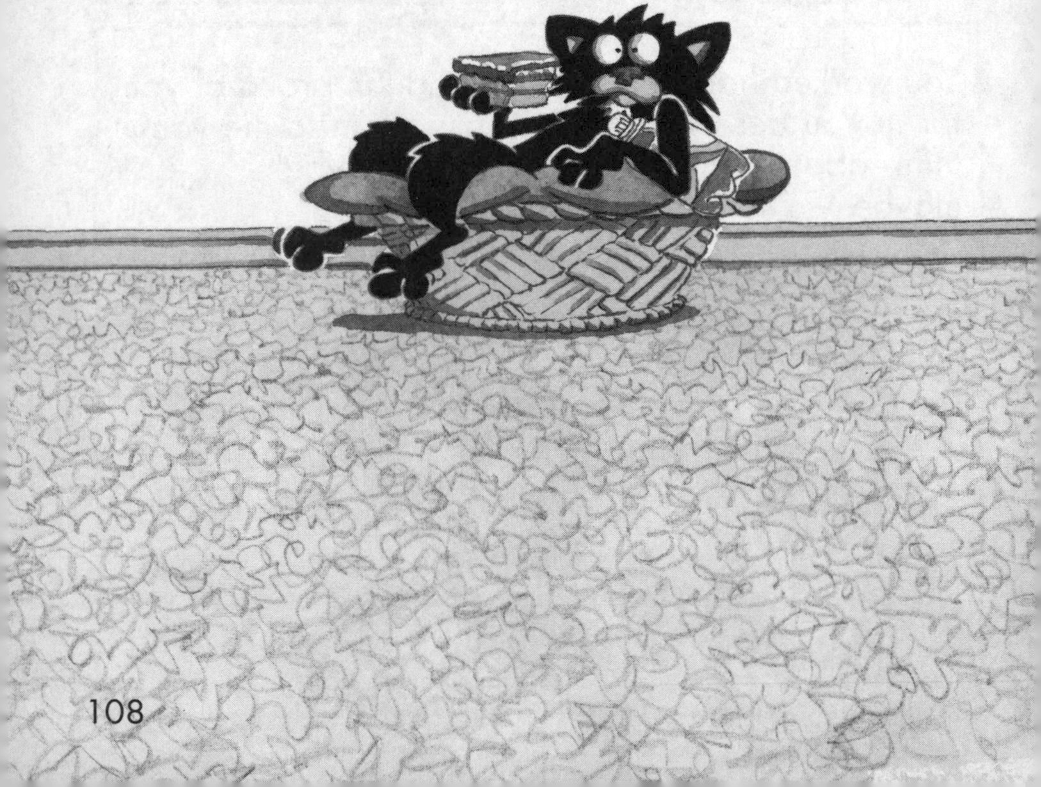

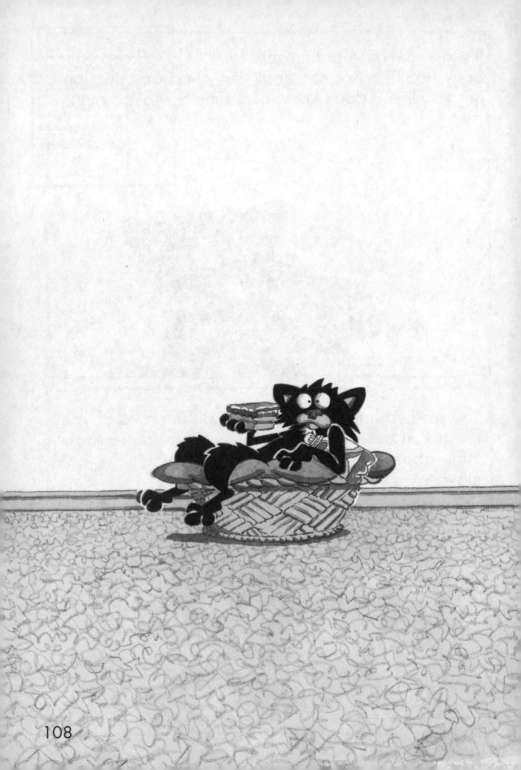

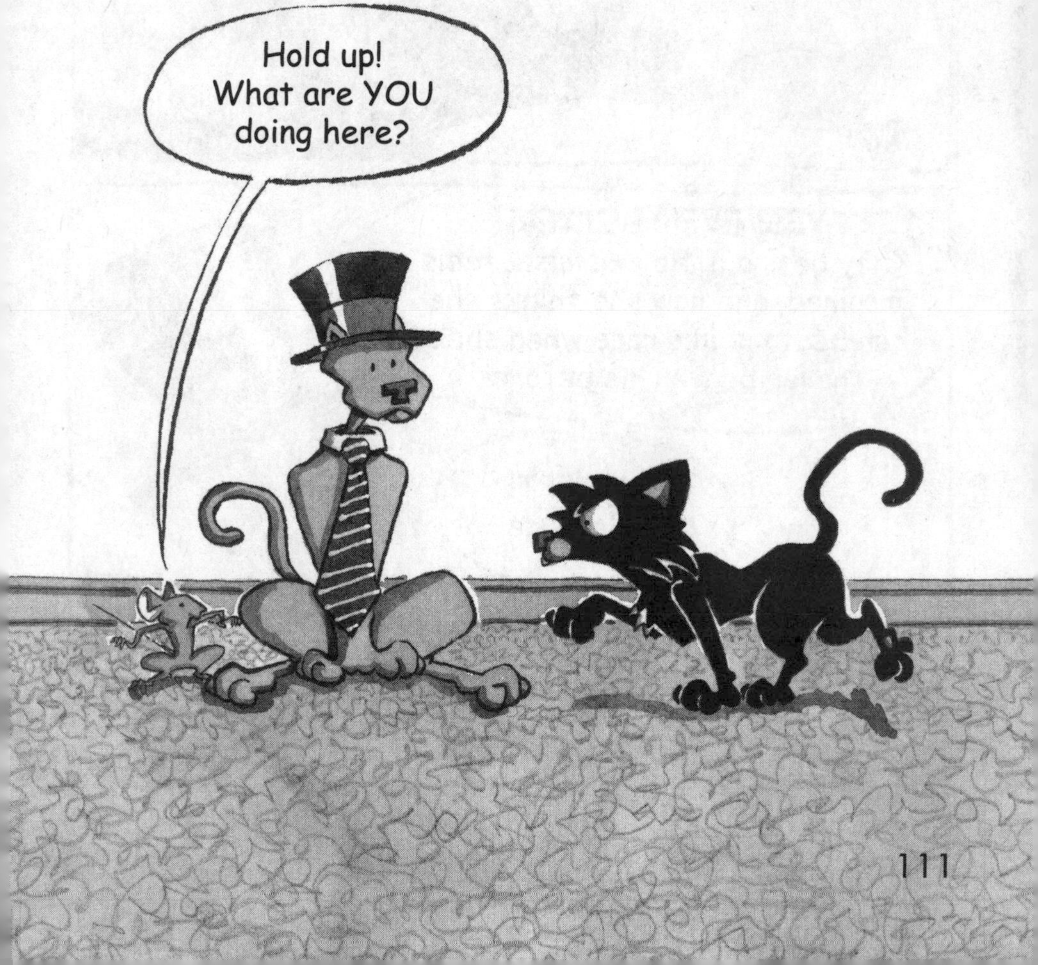
Hold up! What are YOU doing here?

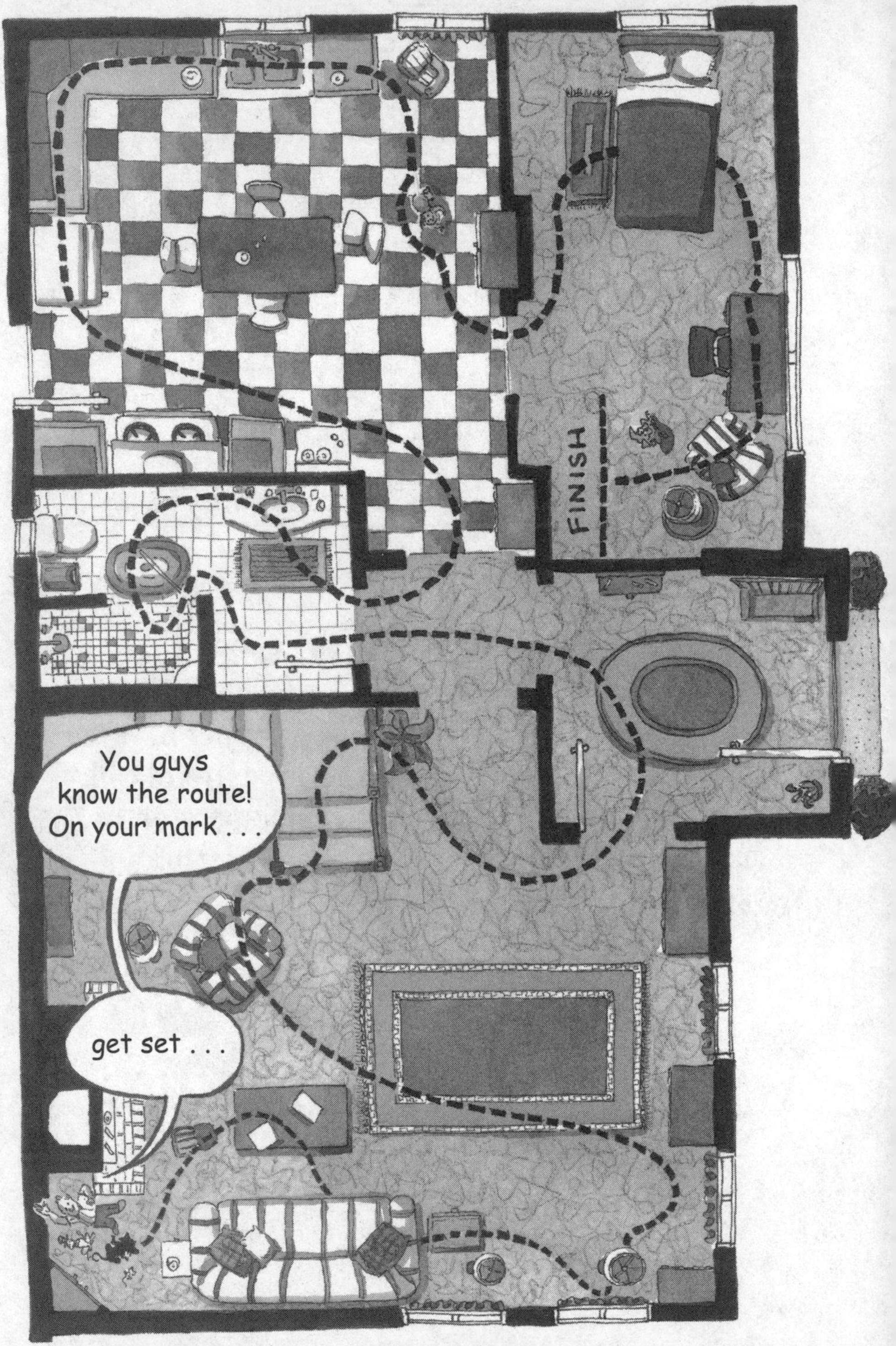
You guys know the route! On your mark . . .
get set . . .
FINISH

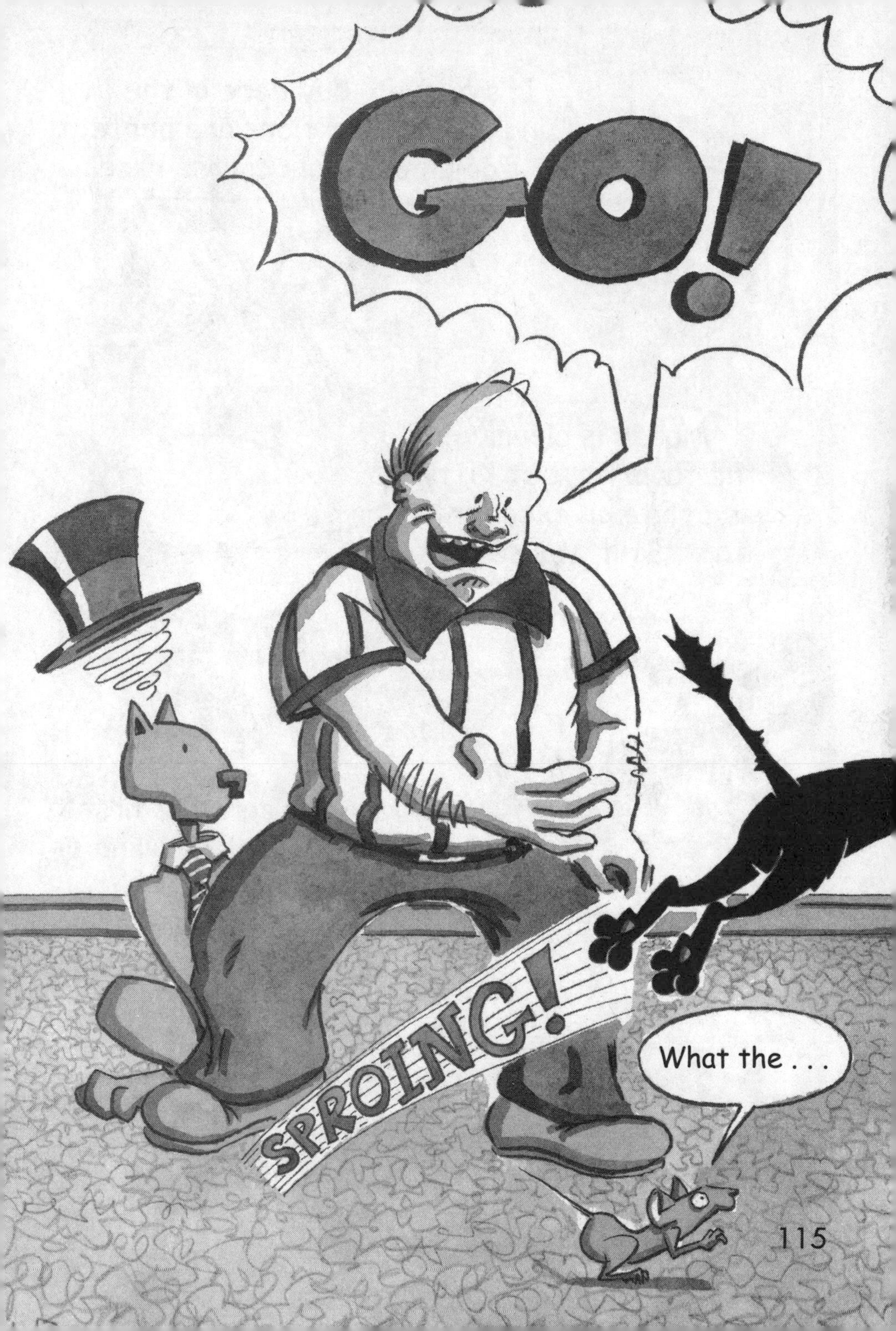
GO!
SPROING!
What the . . .

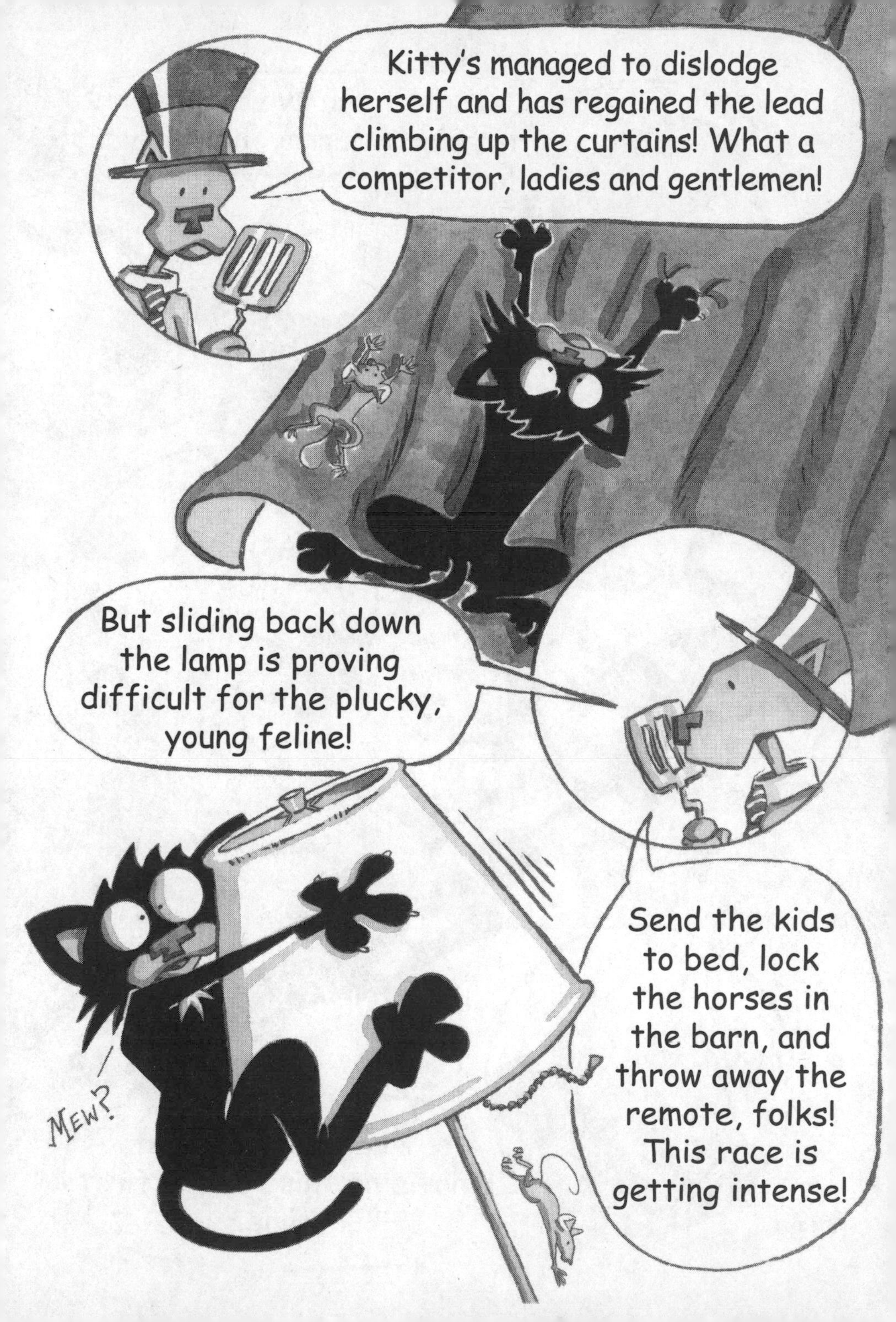
Kitty's managed to dislodge herself and has regained the lead climbing up the curtains! What a competitor, ladies and gentlemen!
But sliding back down the lamp is proving difficult for the plucky, young feline!
Send the kids to bed, lock the horses in the barn, and throw away the remote, folks! This race is getting intense!
MEW?

118

119

120

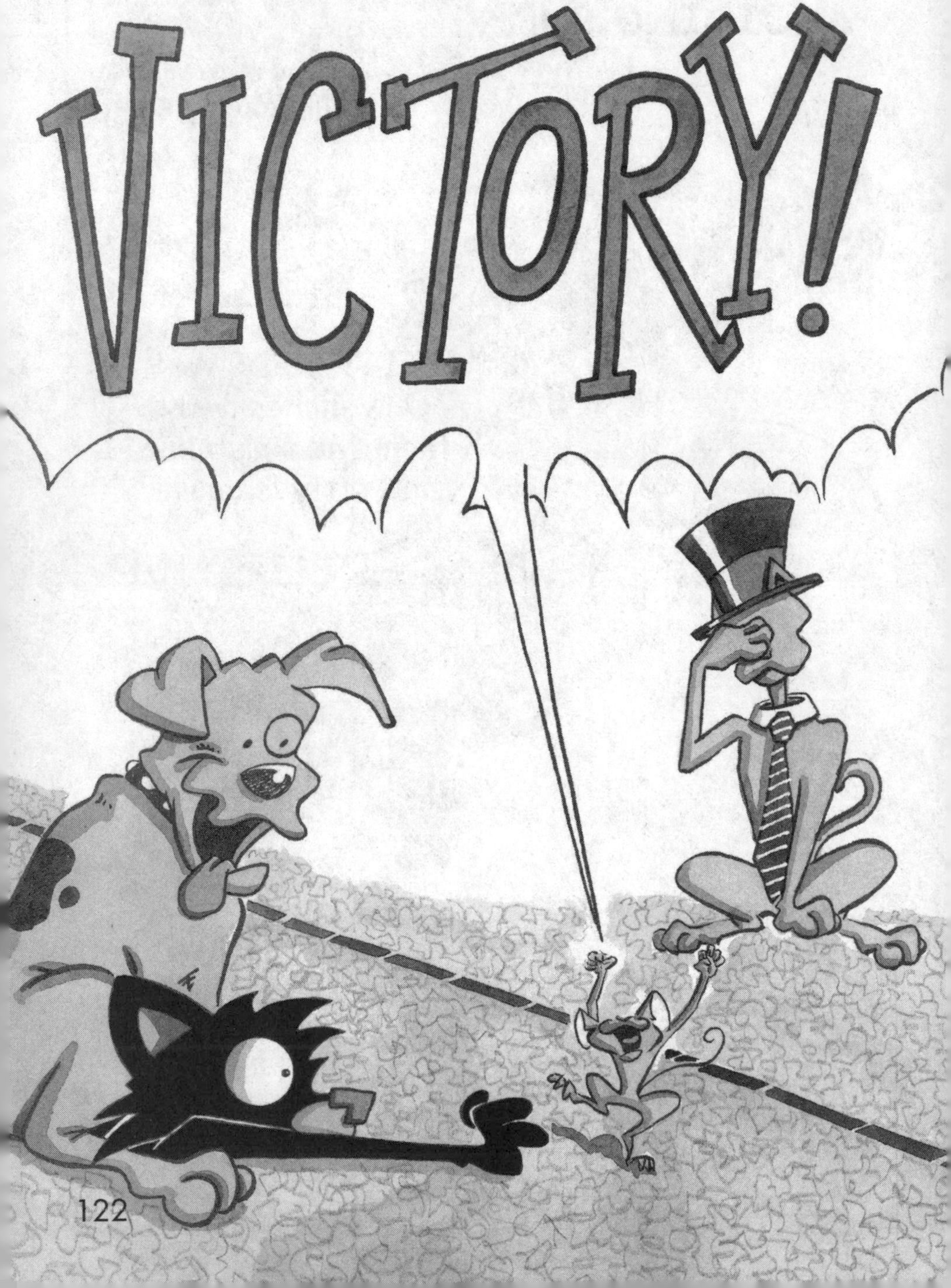
VICTORY!

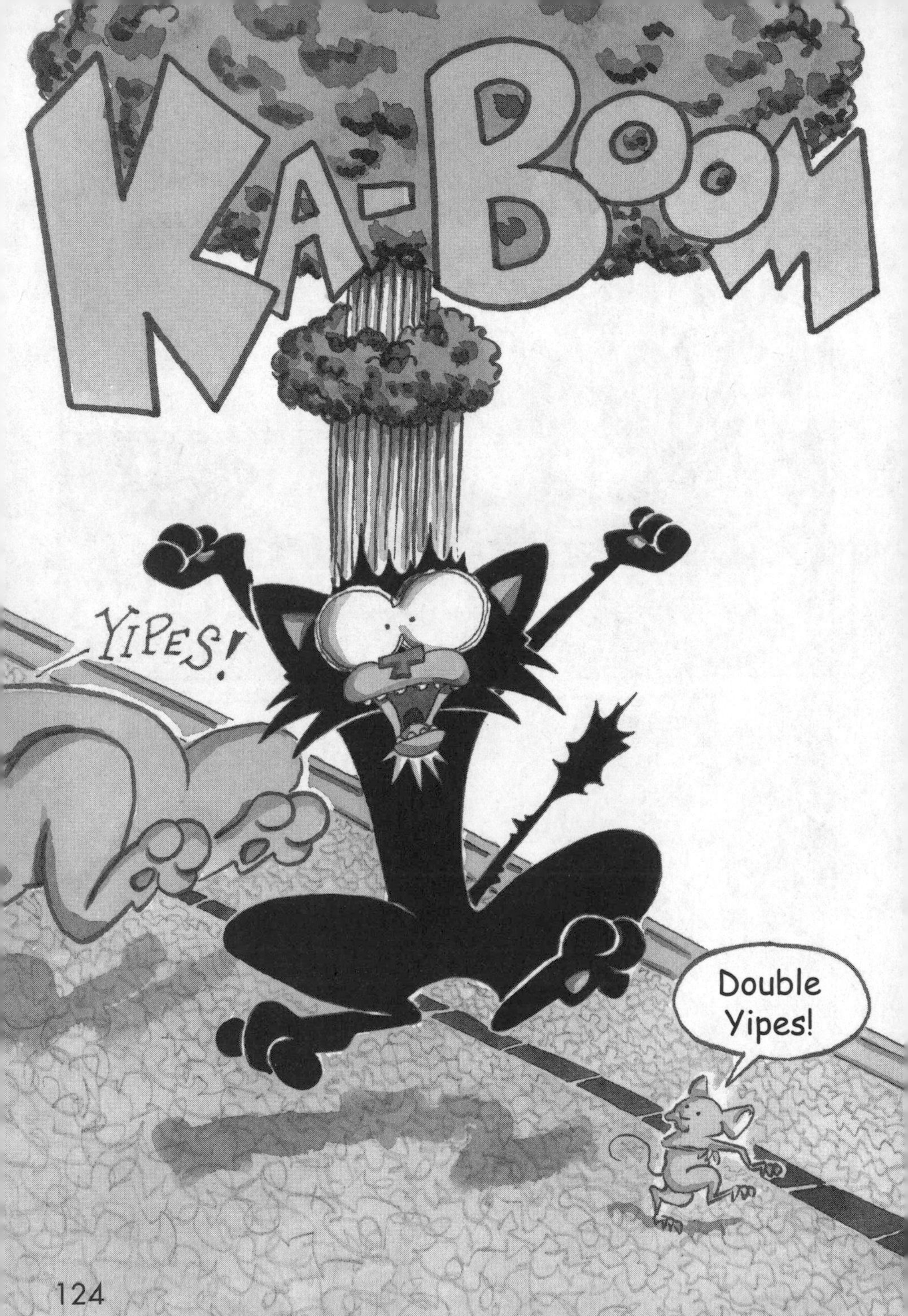
KA-BOOM
YIPES!
Double Yipes!

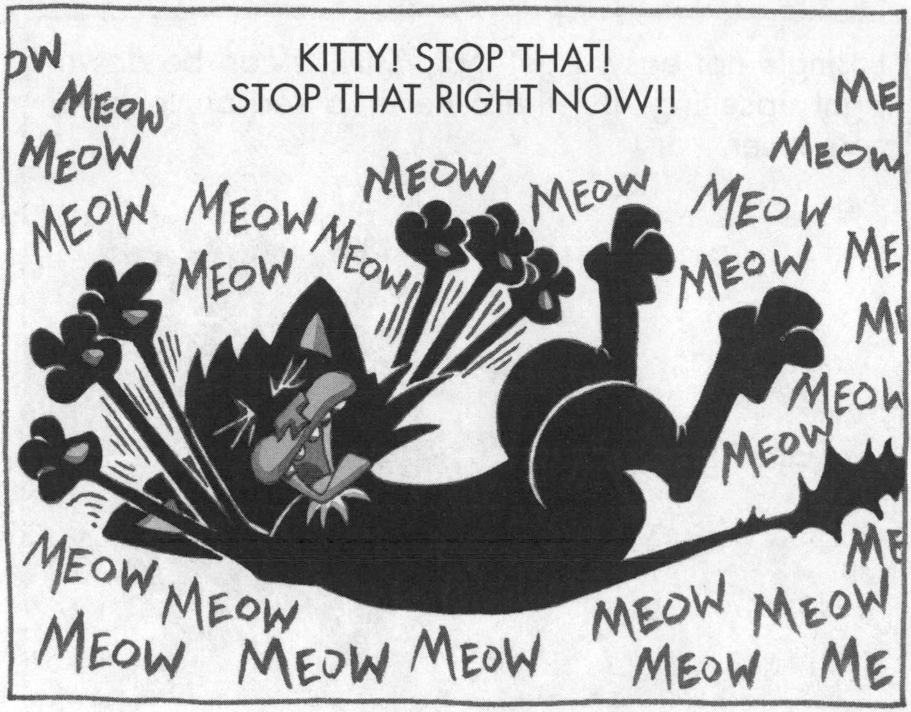
KITTY! STOP THAT!
STOP THAT RIGHT NOW!!
MEOW MEOW MEOW MEOW MEOW MEOW MEOW MEOW MEOW MEOW
MEOW MEOW MEOW MEOW MEOW MEOW MEOW MEOW MEOW MEOW

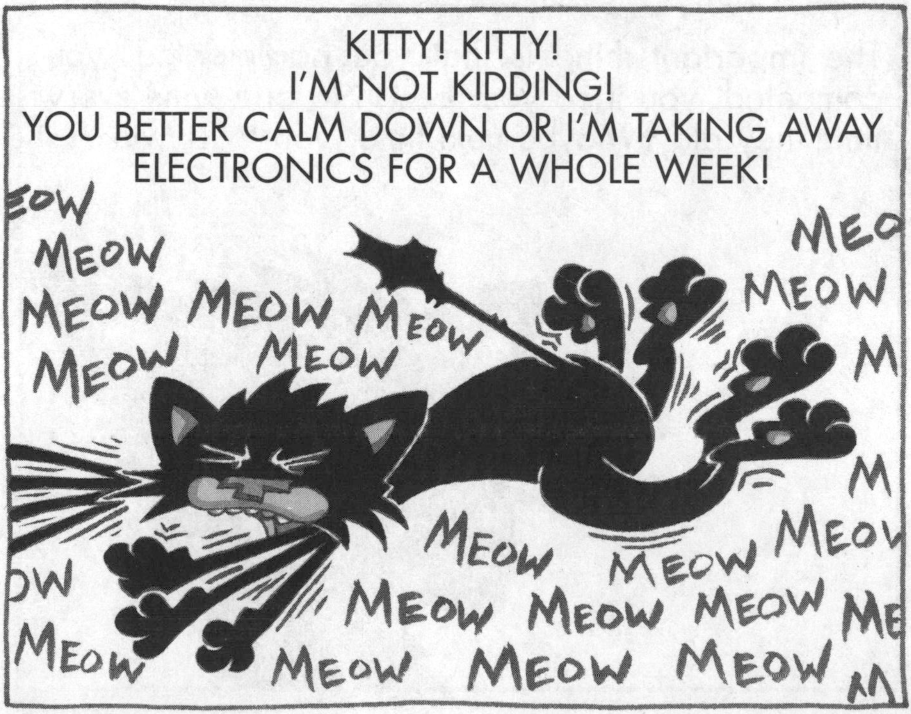
KITTY! KITTY!
I'M NOT KIDDING!
YOU BETTER CALM DOWN OR I'M TAKING AWAY
ELECTRONICS FOR A WHOLE WEEK!
MEOW MEOW MEOW MEOW MEOW MEOW
MEOW MEOW MEOW MEOW MEOW MEOW MEOW MEOW MEOW MEOW

Losing's not easy. I get that, Kitty. It can be down-right upsetting. But that's never a reason to be a sore loser.

The important thing is that you participated, you competed, you tried your best. No one wins every time they play. Maybe next time, you WILL win.

127

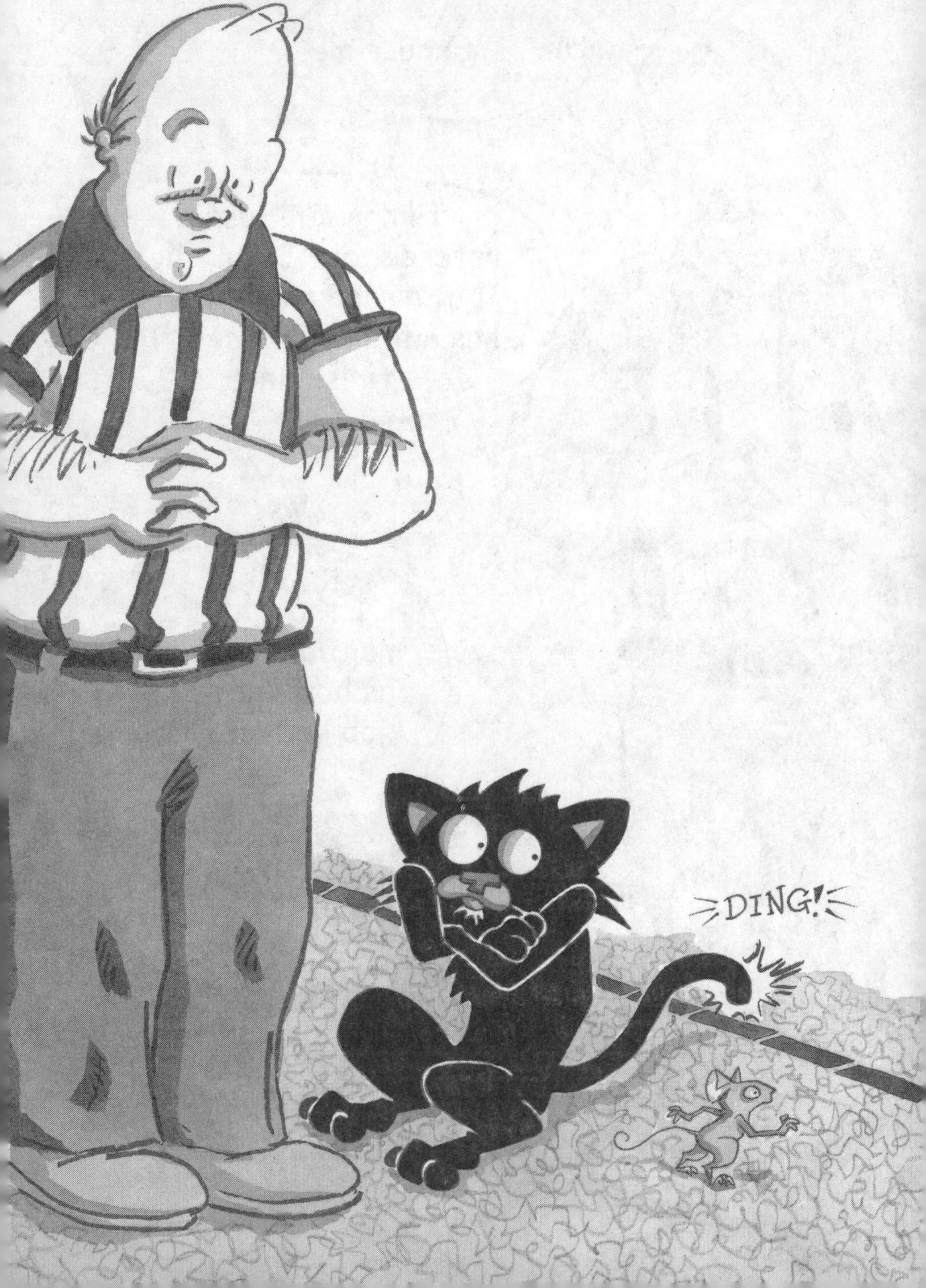
DING!

* Sung to the tune of "We Are the Champions" by Queen.

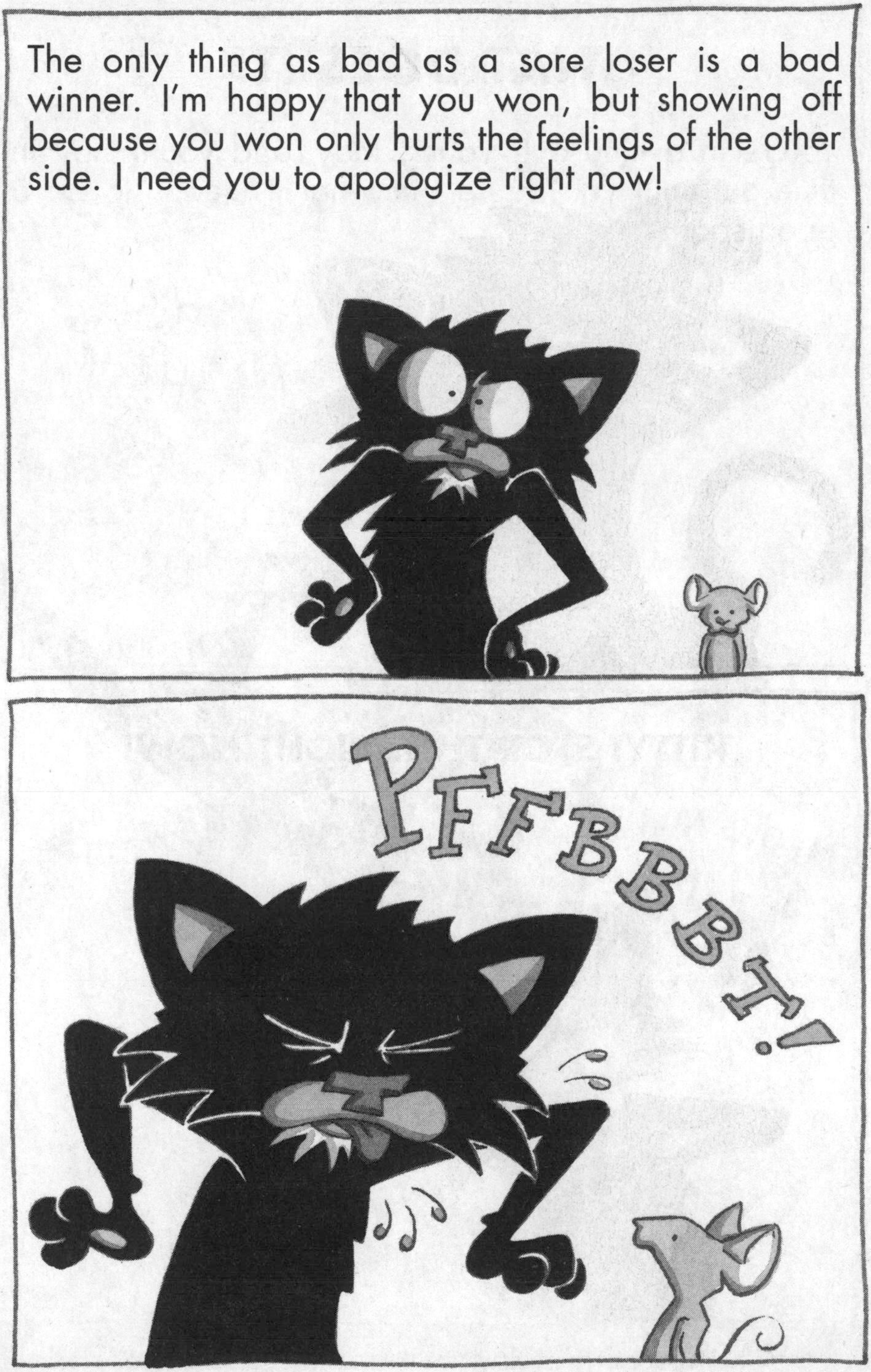
The only thing as bad as a sore loser is a bad winner. I'm happy that you won, but showing off because you won only hurts the feelings of the other side. I need you to apologize right now!
PFFBBBT!

THAT DOES IT!

You're in a time-out, young lady, and you'll stay in time-out until you figure out what it means to be a good sport!

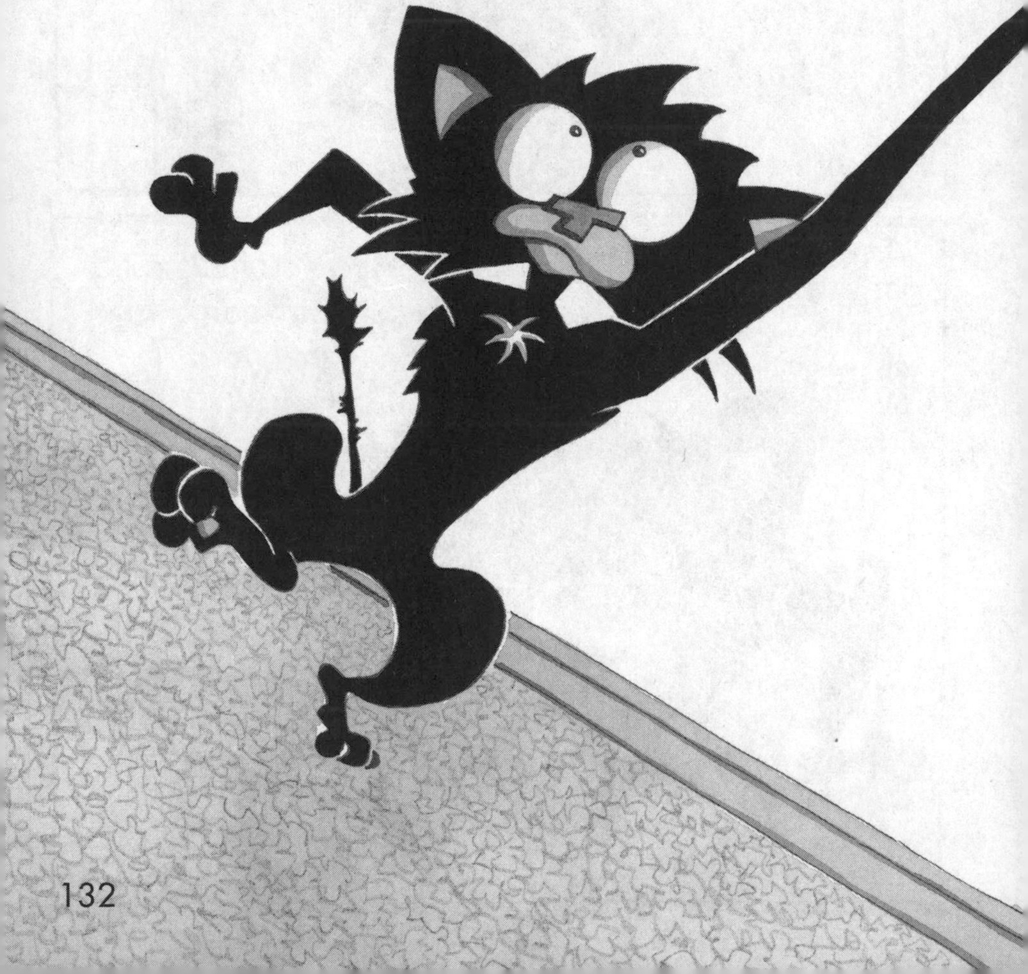

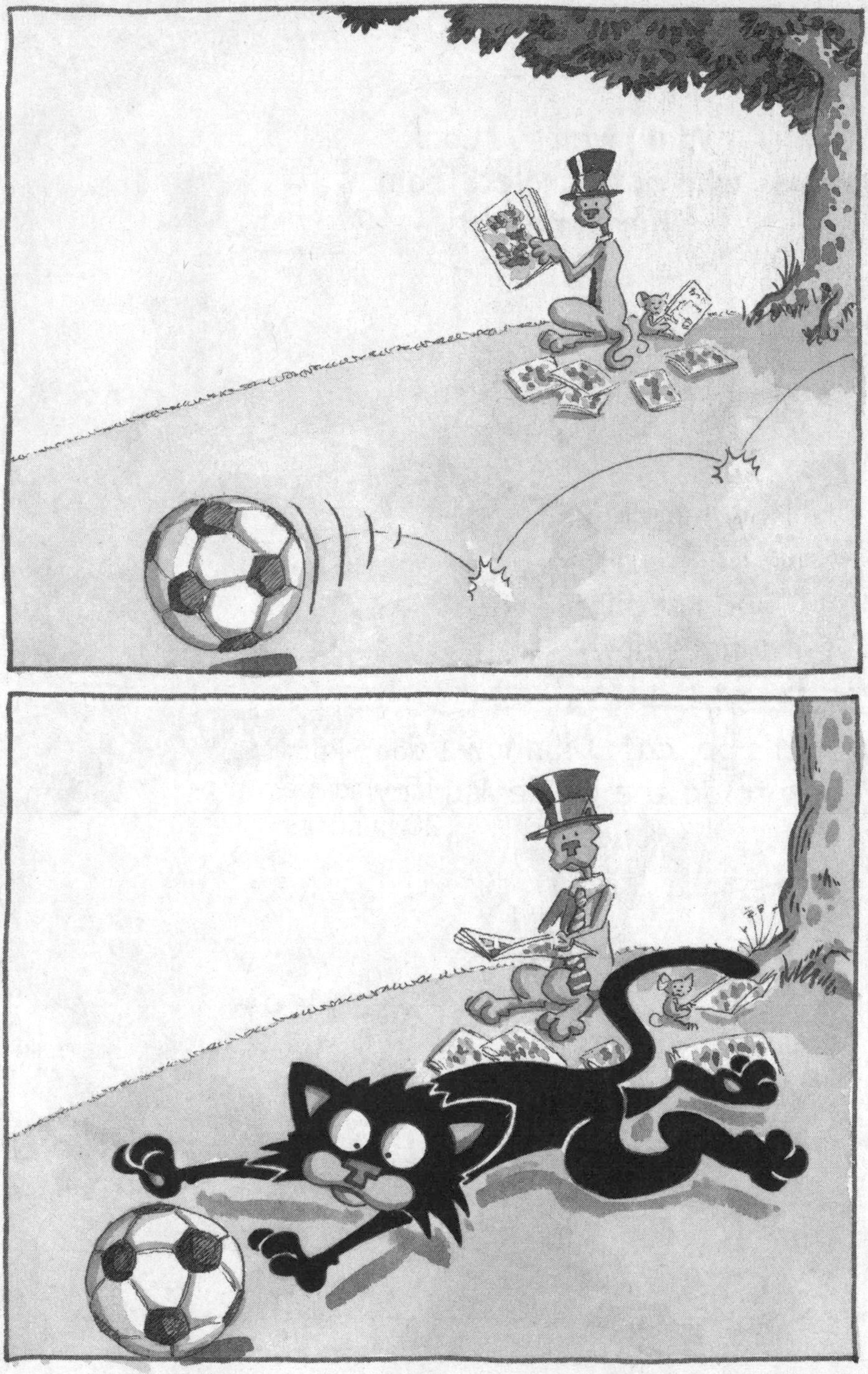

* In England, soccer is called "football." In Italy, it's "calcio." And in Slovenia, it's "nogomet."

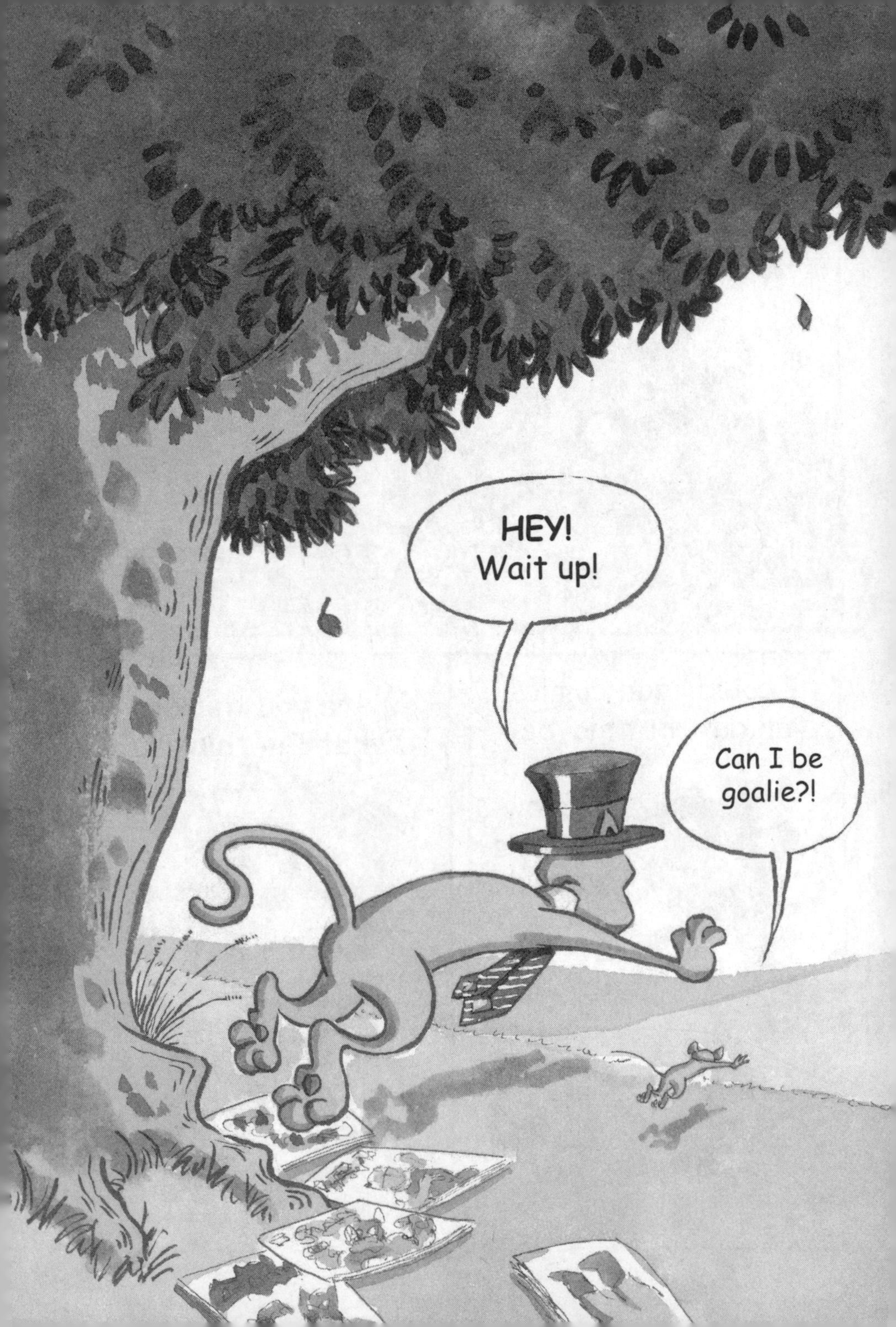
HEY! Wait up!
Can I be goalie?!

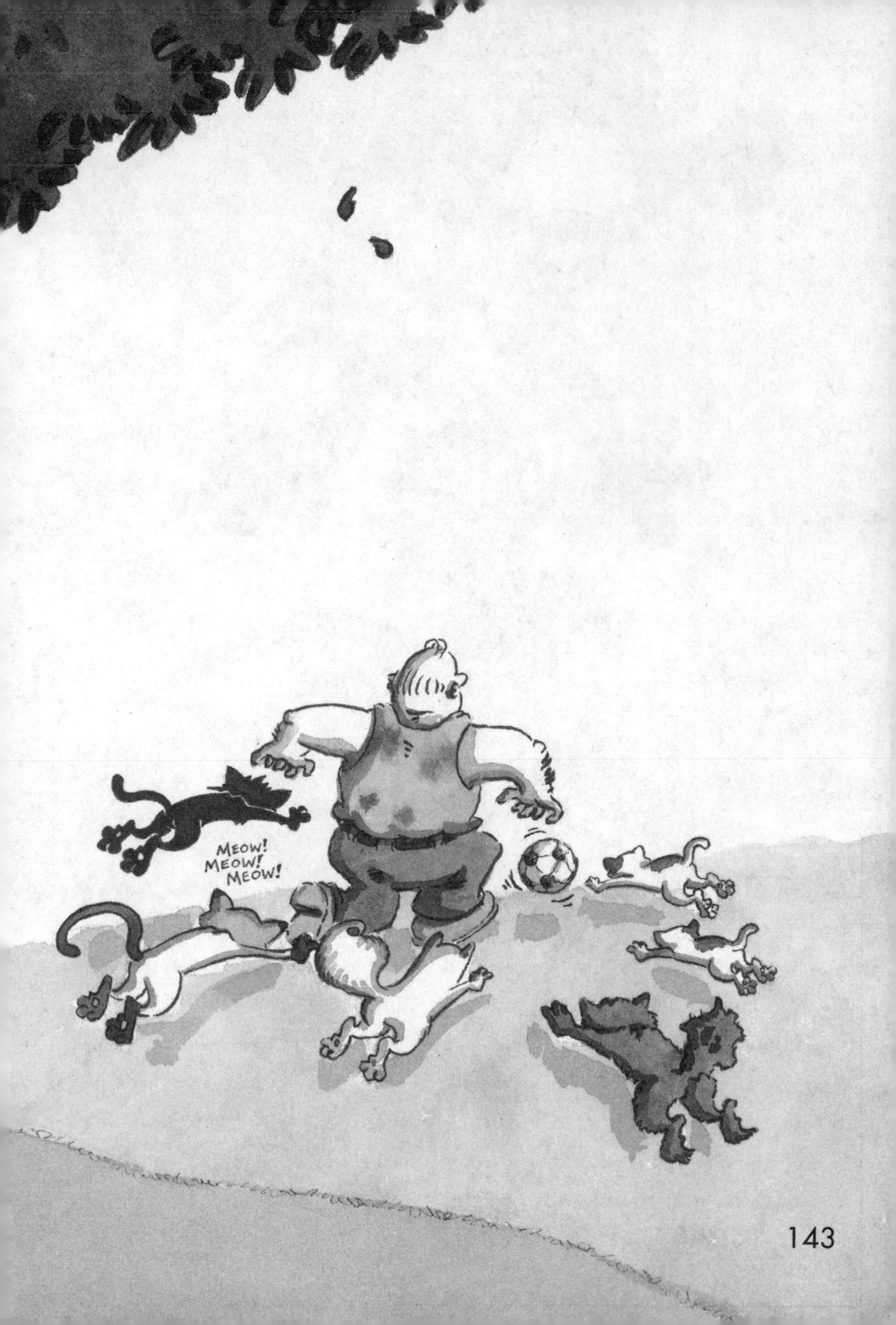
MEOW!
MEOW!
MEOW!

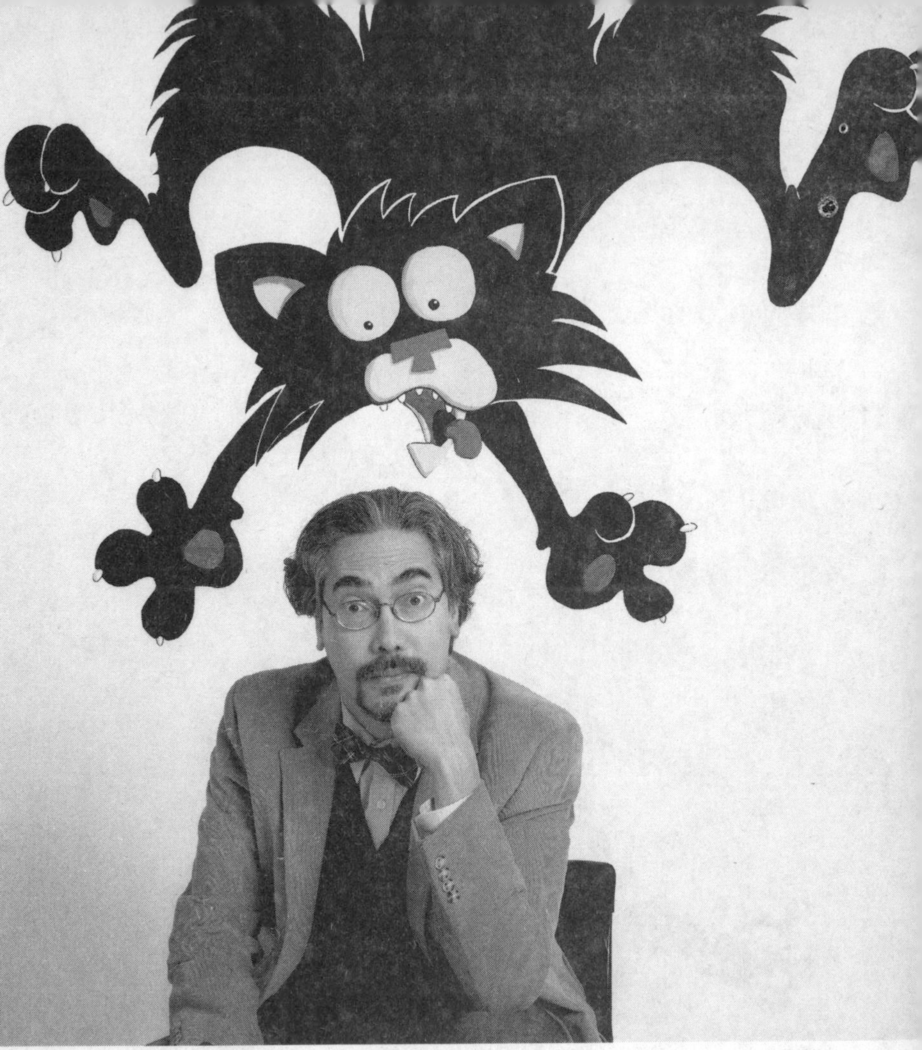

NICK BRUEL is the author and illustrator of the phenomenally successful Bad Kitty series, including the 2012 and 2013 CBC Children's Choice Book Award winners *Bad Kitty Meets the Baby* and *Bad Kitty for President*. Nick has also written and illustrated popular picture books including *A Wonderful Year* and his most recent, *Bad Kitty: Searching for Santa*. Nick lives with his wife and daughter in Westchester, New York. **nickbruel.com**